Wiley was leaning against the low headboard of their platform bed. He was wearing a rugby shirt with stripes of green and tan; the sleeves were pushed up over his forearms.

"Have I seen that shirt before?" Janet asked.

He looked up, surprised. "Maybe not. I think I picked it up in Houston."

He started to read again. She reached over and slipped her hand in the open placket of his shirt, moving her fingertips against him, feeling the warmth of his skin.

"You're making it hard for me to concentrate," he pointed out without taking his eyes off the book.

"I'm sorry," she apologized, and showed her regret by pulling his shirt out of his jeans.

"Mrs. Hunt! I'm reading." Wiley closed the book and started trying to beat her off with it.

He failed utterly.

ABOUT THE AUTHOR

Kathleen Gilles Seidel was born in Lawrence,
Kansas, and attended the University of Chicago
and later the Johns Hopkins University for her
Master's Degree and a Ph.D in English Literature.
For this book on the lives of two workaholics,
Kathy didn't have to look too far from home
to do some research.

Books by Kathleen Gilles Seidel

Chapter One

The stewardess smiled as she recognized the three men boarding the plane. "Two Scotch and waters," she remembered. "One Scotch and soda. Is that right?"

"What can we do?" answered one of the men as he showed her his boarding pass. "Our law firm has one nonconformist beatnik hippie who drinks his Scotch with soda."

"I'm not a beatnik," the soda drinker defended himself. "The beatniks are all grandparents by now. I'm a punk rocker." He pointed to his straight sandy hair. "This is just a wig. I really have a purple Mohawk."

It would be nearly impossible to imagine three men less likely to wear black berets, love beads, or purple Mohawks. They were young, all in their very early thirties, but the suit coats they would doff in a moment were pin-striped with Brooks Brothers labels. Their shirts were white, their ties were dark, their attaché cases were leather, their wedding rings were gold. And since they lived on expense accounts billed to U.S. Oil, they flew first class.

Two of them settled in their seats, forcing Tim Keane, the one professing to have a purple Mohawk, to sit alone on the other side of the aisle. "I'm not sitting next to you," Wiley Hunt informed him as he loosened his tie. "You might have cooties."

"Cooties?" Dan Stewart tightened his seat belt. "What's happened to your vocabulary? I haven't heard anyone talk about cooties since third grade."

"You don't spend enough time with my wife," Wiley answered.

"*You* don't spend enough time with your wife."

"What do you mean? I'm devoted to Mabel."

"Mabel? I thought her name was Hazel."

"Oh, no, I'm sure it's Mabel." Wiley frowned. "Unless it's Mary."

"Wait a minute," Tim put in from across the aisle. "Mary's my wife."

Wiley shook his head. "No. Sarah's your wife. Dan's married to Mary."

"Okay, but if I'm married to Sarah, and Dan's married to Mary, and you've got Mabel-Hazel, who's married to Janet?"

"Janet? Janet who?"

"It doesn't matter," Dan said. "They aren't going to know our names either."

"Well, that's a relief." Tim sighed. "You can't serve divorce papers on a man whose name you can't remember."

The stewardess brought them their drinks, the ice cubes clinking against the thick glass used in the first-class cabin. People flying on U.S. Oil expense accounts weren't expected to drink out of plastic cups. "I haven't seen you three in a while," she said with her professional smile. "You used to be regulars on this run. Are you traveling less?"

"That's certainly one way to put it," Wiley Hunt answered.

Ten months ago the United States Justice Department filed suit against U.S. Oil. It was a complex case, charging that the oil company had spearheaded a conspiracy with other oil companies to fix the bidding on oil leases on federal land, agreeing with one another who would bid on what tract, thus keeping down the cost of the leases. It was a serious action and the company had immediately hired Hastings & Clark, a law firm in Washington, D.C., that specialized in representing large companies before the federal government.

Dan Stewart, Tim Keane, and Wiley Hunt, associate attorneys at the firm, had been assigned to the case. At first they did much of their work in Washington, flying out to Houston only a few times a month. Then as the case grew more complex, they began staying in Houston all week, every week, flying in on Sunday night and out on Friday night. That's when the stewardess started remembering them.

But by fall they weren't always coming home on the weekends either; as Wiley said, they weren't traveling, they were virtually living in Houston. In November something had come up at the last minute and they had all missed Thanksgiving.

Dan had at least made it home for Christmas, but of the three, only he was a father. His wife—who was, by the way, Sarah, not Janet, Mary, or the mythic Mabel-Hazel—had given birth to their first baby in October. Christmas had been the fifth time Dan had seen his daughter.

Wiley and Tim, figuring that their wives had gone home to their respective parents, had skipped the holiday altogether.

These yuletide efforts had resulted in Hastings & Clark pulling a surprise move on December 26th, something the government was so unprepared for that the judge had been forced to rule in the oil company's favor. It had been an important procedural question, and by the end of January, the United States government threw its collective hands up and settled the suit out of court. The Justice Department lawyers still believed U.S. Oil was guilty, but acknowledged—quite privately, of course—that that there wasn't a thing to do about it, not with the brigades of Hastings & Clark attorneys forever storming across the horizon, armed with obscure citations, century-old precedents, and U.S. Oil's willingness to pay heart-stopping legal bills.

So the three senior associates turned their files over to the younger people for the final winding down of the case, and they were now leaving Houston for what they hoped would be forever, flying back to their homes and to their wives, who probably did remember their names but who weren't necessarily happy about it.

For all their fine legal skills, for all their analytic powers and reasoning abilities, not one of these men had the sense to realize how their wives had resented their absence. When the three were joking about divorce papers, they had considered themselves joking.

In fact, as they were sitting comfortably in the wide blue seats of the first-class compartment, with their ties loosened and their jackets off, drinking their Scotch, and examining the menus the stewardess had handed them, they felt quite marvelous about themselves. Downright smug, in fact. After all, they had done such a splendid job. They had won, and now they felt as confident as law-firm associates can feel—that they would be rewarded with partnerships in the firm.

A partnership would mean security, power, and financial ease; it was the goal each had been working for since leaving law school six years before. That's what they had told their wives last summer when the women had complained about them never being home. "This is my chance, my chance to make partner." And to their minds, that excused every absence, every neglect.

Being made partner was so important that they didn't even notice when their wives stopped complaining.

When the No Smoking light flicked off, Tim Keane leaned his seat back. He laced his fingers behind his sandy head and looked across the aisle at Wiley Hunt. "What are you going to do next week?"

"Sail," Wiley answered. "I'd like to go sailing. Down to the Caribbean, maybe."

"I thought Janet didn't like to sail," Dan remarked.

"She's not crazy about it," Wiley admitted. "She thinks it's boring."

"Boring? How can anyone from the Midwest think something boring?"

"But who would be better qualified to know

boring than a Midwesterner?" Tim asked. "They must be experts. You know how the Eskimos are supposed to have seven words for snow or something like that? Midwesterners must have twenty words for boring. If Janet Hunt thinks something is boring, I'll believe her."

"I don't know," Dan disagreed. "She married Wiley, didn't she? I think he's boring."

"So does she," Wiley put in. "She thinks I'm very boring. It's just that she likes being bored. When she gets homesick, she runs out and gets bored. Then she feels like she's in Missouri again. That's why she had to marry a lawyer, to be sure of a steady source of boredom."

"Do you emit little green boring-cooties?" Tim asked.

"She says so," Wiley said modestly.

Wiley Hunt did not, of course, believe a word he was saying. It never crossed his mind that his wife did not treasure his company. So he was surprised, angry, even a little hurt, when a few hours later she vetoed the sailing plan. "I can't just pick up and leave," she said.

"You'd think," he said tightly, "that after ten months of this case, you could take a day or so off now that I'm home."

"We've got two big pitches next week." Janet Hunt was senior writer at a local advertising agency. "There's no way I can leave now. If you had given me some notice—"

"Notice? How was I to know when they'd settle?"

"Well, then, there's no one to blame. But it

can't be helped. I simply can't take time off now; maybe sometime in the spring I can. If you need to get away, you should go on alone."

"That would certainly be boatloads of fun."

Later in the evening Wiley spoke to his father, who was one of the senior partners at a New York law firm that was even larger and—if possible—more conservative than Hastings & Clark. Surprisingly, his father had also had a case just settled. So the two of them went off to the Caribbean together.

And when Wiley returned ten days later, he discovered how fortunate he had been. Janet hadn't wanted to go sailing with him. Sarah Stewart and Mary Keane hadn't wanted to stay married.

Dan Stewart had gone from the airport to an eerily silent house. Sarah had taken the baby back to her parents in Boston without telling him, having decided that a man who never saw his family didn't deserve to have one. And Tim Keane was confronted with the delightful news that his wife as well was moving out of their home; she was having an affair with a lawyer over at the Environmental Protection Agency and wanted to be free to continue seeing him.

"That's some swell tan." Tim Keane had just stepped into Wiley's office on the latter's first day back at work.

"I know." Wiley ran a hand through his sun-streaked hair. "It's embarrassing; I look like such a ne'er-do-well."

Attorneys at Hastings & Clark did not get suntans. A suntan was suspect. If you showed up at the office on Monday morning with a tan, it meant you hadn't spent the weekend working.

"Did you have a good time? You went with your father, didn't you?"

"Yes, I did—both have a good time and go with him."

"Aren't those synonymous? Don't you always enjoy being with him?"

"Of course."

"Because you could talk about law the whole time?"

"Of course."

Wiley's mother had died just as he was starting law school, but father and son still saw each other frequently—thereby giving themselves the pleasure of having exactly the same sort of intimate discussions that they had with their professional associates.

"By the way," Wiley asked, "where's Dan? I didn't see him."

"He went up to Boston over the weekend. Maybe he's not back yet." Tim took off his glasses, and as he was polishing the lenses with his handkerchief, he spoke without looking at Wiley. "You did hear about all the fun fireworks that have been happening here?"

Wiley nodded. "Janet told me last night. I'm sorry, Tim."

It wasn't at all odd that Wiley and Tim had chatted about other matters first or that Tim should speak of his shattered marriage as "fun fireworks." That was the way they did things.

"Well, I can't say that I'm crazy about it,"

Tim concurred. "And I can't figure out what to do. I remember learning about fee-splitting in law school, but not this."

"You must have cut that class."

"Maybe I did." Tim got up and crossed Wiley's office, seeming, for the moment, very interested in the floor-to-ceiling bookcases, in the green-bound volumes and the neatly stacked copies of the Federal Register. "You know what was particularly fun? I saw them at lunch together last week. I don't know...he had his hand on the back of her chair. I thought I would..." Tim turned abruptly, flicking his hand. "But that's insane. Why should I care if he has his hand on the back of her chair when you consider everything else he has done?"

Wiley didn't say anything. There wasn't anything to say.

"At least you're being spared this," Tim went on. "I take it that Janet didn't have any little bombshell to drop on you."

"Who? Janet?" Wiley shook his head, then realized how complacent he must sound. "Who would have ever thought that one day I would be grateful for having married a Midwesterner?"

Tim did laugh. "Probably not you."

Wiley's phone rang and Tim started to leave. Wiley picked up the receiver, but covered the mouthpiece. "Do you want to meet for a drink after work?"

Tim started to nod, but the conversation about Mary and Janet had made him sensitive. "There's no reason for that. You go on home."

Wiley understood what Tim was saying and shook his head. "Janet never gets home until seven or so; I'll see you around six."

They met that evening in the front lobby. As benefited the character of Hastings & Clark, the firm's offices were decorated in sedate, expensive fashion. The dark oak floors of the lobby were covered with Oriental carpets; the receptionist sat behind an English writing table beneath oil portraits of the long-dead Messrs. Hastings and Clark.

"Well, how does it feel to be back in the salt mines?" Tim asked.

"I hated every minute of it," Wiley returned. Both Tim and he loved their work.

As they waited for the elevator Wiley went on, "I got assigned a FalCon case today."

"You did!" Tim's blue eyes sparkled behind the lenses of his glasses. "That *is* good news."

Falport Consolidated Chemical Industries was one of Hastings & Clark's oldest clients. People who were going to be passed over in the partnership election next September did not get assigned FalCon cases.

"Of course, it's nothing big," Wiley added. "Just a routine toxic waste case. Some farmer in Iowa claims that one of FalCon's subsidiaries is dumping some chemical on his land. He has almost no evidence; the entire case seems based on the fact that he saw a truck go by. Even his neighbors say he's crazed. But we'll probably settle with him anyway, just to keep it out of court . . . and the papers. The media loves toxic waste stories."

"Well, better you than me." Tim was pleased enough with his own new assignments that he didn't envy Wiley a FalCon case. "Mary hates it when I—" He stopped.

Wiley knew what he was about to say. *Mary hates it when I have a toxic waste case.*

Mary Keane was a public-interest attorney. In fact, it had been during an environmental pollution case that she had met the EPA lawyer who was now putting his hand on the back of her chair—and other places.

But the disputes between Hastings & Clark on one side and EPA and public-interest lawyers on the other went beyond who put his hands where. There was no question that Hastings & Clark represented many of the nation's prime industrial pollutors. Of course, the firm would have defended itself—if such a firm ever felt compelled to defend itself—by saying that they were simply trying to help their clients obey the rapidly changing laws. Many times a company would initiate a practice long before it was illegal or known to be dangerous. Hastings & Clark tried to help its client find a way to conform to each new regulation without going bankrupt—a fate that some of the regulations seemed designed to ensure.

These were all very complex issues which marriage had a way of reducing to the most simplistic. Wiley knew that when Mary was angry with Tim, she used to attack the firm and what they all did there. Tim had never liked it when she did that...but he probably liked it more than what she was doing now.

The bar the two attorneys entered was quiet but crowded, full of typical Washington people.

People who had no other life but their work, whose professional colleagues were the closest they had to family or friends, who were all a little depressed when the weekend arrived. Wiley and Tim would fit right in.

Wiley looked at the crowd. "We'll never get a table. Shall we go somewhere else?"

"No, I see someone who will let us sit with her. At least she'll let *me* sit with her."

"Oh?" Wiley was surprised. True, Mary had moved out, but when on earth did Tim find time to meet women?

Tim understood. "I'm flattered, but no such luck. It's Janet."

"Janet? My Janet?"

"I don't think you are allowed to say things like that anymore, Wiley. She's not your Janet."

"You know what I mean. Is she here?"

"Over there." Tim pointed.

Indeed it was Janet. The soft feathery layers of her earth-brown hair gleamed under the bar's green-shaded lamps. She was sitting with four men: two of them were strangers to Wiley and the other two were the founders of the agency she worked at, Michael Champion and Alan Rule. Of those two, Wiley respected Michael Champion, who ran the business end of the agency. He thought Alan Rule, the tall, thin creative director, was half-crazed.

As Tim and he approached the table Michael Champion noticed them and called.

And Wiley saw that before he had called to them, Champion had first taken his hand off the back of Janet's chair.

The back of her . . . Good God, surely not.

"Well, hello," Alan, the creative director, sang out, and he started to hum some bouncy tune that Wiley couldn't place.

Tim apparently recognized the tune Alan was humming and began to laugh, and Janet elbowed Alan hard, telling him to shut up. She stood up and hastily started introducing everyone, identifying the two strangers as clients. ". . . and this is my husband, Wiley," she finished.

That's right . . . your husband.

One of the clients—Roger Rose was his name—started. "As in Wiley Hunt?"

"Yes," Alan answered for him. "Isn't it cute? Janet uses his name. She's the last woman of her generation to do so."

The last woman . . . yes, yes, she'd be the last woman to . . .

Rose turned to him. "So you must be Wiley, Jr.?"

Wiley blinked and, taking one of the chairs Tim had captured from another table, tried to concentrate on what the other man was saying. "No, I'm not. My father and I have different middle initials. He's Wiley D. I'm Wiley L."

He had said that countless times, and as he was saying it again, it occurred to Wiley that these two clients of Janet's must be lawyers. Wiley D. Hunt was hardly a household word; most Americans had never heard of his father, nor did they have any idea of the extent to which his work in securities law affected their lives. But other lawyers knew.

So these two must be lawyers and Janet had introduced them as clients. They had hired an ad agency.

Oh, sure, advertising wasn't unethical any-more—the Bar Association had changed their rule a few years back—but still it seemed so, well, so unseemly for lawyers to advertise. Hastings & Clark would never dream of it. A single line in the Yellow Pages, a listing in the Martindale-Hubble legal directory, but that was it.

Firms like Hastings & Clark have a certain style, a manner of dignity, restraint, and poise. Earning a partnership involved more than proving stamina, intelligence, and dedication. A partner had to fit in; he had to wear the right ties, drink the right Scotch, use the right pen. And he had to have poise and presence. A partner had to be able to tell clients of multimillion-dollar judgments against them; he had to sit down to dinner with men who hated everything he represented, and he had to do it all with an unshakable assurance you can't buy at Brooks Brothers.

Wiley Hunt had the right style, and why wouldn't he? He had learned from the best—his father.

But part of the style was not to let the contempt for other lawyers show, but to act instead like these guys settling little personal injury claims and doing real estate closings—lawyers who *advertised*, for heaven's sake—and who were in the same business as Hastings & Clark.

"Actually," Tim said, obviously careful not to look at Wiley, careful not to exchange a superior glance—Tim had the right style too—"it would seem more honest if he were 'junior.' Then everyone would know that our firm has only the markdown version of Wiley Hunt, not the real thing."

"What firm is that?" the other client asked.

"Hastings & Clark."

"Oh."

Tim began asking the other two lawyers about their firm, his voice carefully bleached of all condescension, and as they talked, Wiley looked over at Janet.

She was sitting between Michael and Alan. That seemed wrong to him. If this was a friendly drink with two clients, the agency people shouldn't cluster together. Janet certainly shouldn't be sitting next to Michael Champion. Oh, well, advertising was more casual about things than law firms were—especially this agency.

At least Champion had gotten Janet and Alan to start dressing like human beings. Alan used to show up at the office in Hawaiian shirts, and Wiley had seen Janet leave for work in a denim skirt, knee socks, and a down vest over a white turtleneck. But as the agency grew successful and got more reputable clients, Champion had been emphatic: Janet and Alan were to look like grown-ups. "Dress like Wiley does," Champion had told her, and she had done so, wearing, at least on the days they were seeing clients, dark suits and white blouses. Even the ties she sometimes bowed beneath the slender ruffle of her collar had the same patterns as the ties in his closet.

He liked her looking that way. It made her look successful—which, of course, she was. And surely it made her life easier. In the old days it seemed like Janet couldn't walk down a street alone without being interrupted. Teenagers asked her directions; men asked her to take their daughters to the ladies' room; everytime she went near the Mall, tourists asked her to take their picture while they stood in front of the Capitol or one of the monuments. She had had such a friendly, approachable air to her; she seemed like the sort of person you could trust with your camera or your daughter.

A pin-striped suit protected a person from all that. Not that Janet ever seemed to mind the things complete strangers asked her to do, but Wiley minded in her behalf.

Which wasn't all he would mind... Michael Champion moving his gray-suited arm... Was it possible?

Well, it made a certain amount of sense—that Champion might try, that is. After all, the agency needed Janet, and Michael must know her well. He would know that she was incapable of distinguishing friendship from business. Like too many women, she would allow her talents to be exploited if she thought the people doing it needed and liked her.

And wasn't that a way to show her that she was needed and liked?

Well, Michael might try and Janet wouldn't mind the hand on the back of her chair, the extra kiss on her cheek, but she wouldn't...

Or would she? Tim's wife had.

Wiley glanced at his watch. "Janet, are you ready to go home? Or do you have to go back to the office?"

"No, I can leave." She turned to Tim, who

had stood when she did. She put a hand on his arm. "We didn't get a chance to talk. How are you?"

"Never better."

Janet did not look convinced, and in a quick moment Tim covered her hand with his own, pressing it against his arm, showing her that he understood, that he appreciated her concern. But his perfect-lawyer expression did not change.

Wiley nodded a farewell to Tim and shook hands with Janet's two clients.

He asked her about them as soon as they were outside. "They're lawyers, aren't they?"

She nodded, her brown eyes alert, perhaps laughing. She knew what he was about to say.

But he said it anyway. "So why did they come to you?"

"You can have three guesses, and I'll even give you a hint. We're an advertising agency."

"Surely it's not for late-night TV spots."

"It certainly is," and at his groan, she went on. "Oh, Wiley, don't be such a snob. They're trying to do something important, to get people to come in for legal services before it's too late. They want ads that are reassuring without being threatening—so that they seem like the Marcus Welbys of law."

That was so typical of her, Wiley thought, that the minute she needed some sort of figurative speech, she dredged up an old TV show.

"It's a problem," Janet continued. "We don't want to shoot them in front of a bunch of law books like all the other ads, but they're too to look authoritative in other settings

She trailed off as if she believed he wasn't interested.

Well, he wasn't, and he wasn't going to pretend like he was.

In a moment she spoke again. "It seems odd, running into you like that. I guess I still think of you as being out of town."

"I hope to be in Washington a lot more now."

"And I suppose you're going to want to do all sorts of weird stuff like eat dinner together."

"It would be nice."

Even before U.S. Oil had turned Wiley into a blank space on the canvas of their marriage, the two of them had long since abandoned any settled routine about dinner. One or the other would have to work late so often that it was pointless to make plans in the morning. If they managed to get phone calls through each other's secretaries in the late afternoon, they might coordinate something, whether eating in a restaurant or out of their own microwave, but more often than not they didn't manage that.

"Do we have anything at home?" Wiley asked.

"Of course."

He stepped off the curb to hail a cab, but Janet grabbed his arm, stopping him.

"You're home now," she reminded him. "You aren't living on an expense account anymore. It's the subway for you."

He grimaced. They had lived lavishly in Houston. They had used limousines and booked hotel suites. Room service had delivered their meals and pressed their suits. The Justice Department lawyers, trying to make it on their government per diems, couldn't even order wine with dinner, but the Hastings & Clark attorneys had not had to think about their daily expenses. U.S. Oil was not interested in having its legal talent squander energy worrying about the price of a room-service breakfast. The company's legal troubles were worry enough.

So it was going to be a little hard to adjust to being an ordinary human being again.

The subway was crowded, and they both had to stand. Janet, small enough that she couldn't reach the overhead bar comfortably, leaned against Wiley, holding on to his lapel when the train swayed. He could smell the vanilla scent of her cologne. She must have put more on late in the afternoon; otherwise it would have worn off by now.

"Janet."

She looked up.

"When we came into the bar, what was that song Rule was whistling?"

Her eyes danced beneath her dark lashes. "You didn't recognize it?"

She was flirting with him. "No."

"Tim did."

"I know." Although Janet did not talk about cooties, part of her did seem, at least to her husband, permanently mired in popular culture. She always recognized old hits; she remembered the names of all the characters on the old *Dick Van Dyke Show;* she knew which pinball machines were Gottliebs and which were Ballys. He sometimes thought it was the result of having every Friday and Saturday night of h school years driving around in cars; her memory for such trivia was, he suspected, the first stages of carbon monoxide poisoning.

"What was it?" he repeated.

"The Angels recorded it. Ronstadt sang it at a concert after Jerry Brown—"

"Janet, I don't care about that. What's the title?"

"'My Boyfriend's Back.'"

"Oh, terrific."

"What's wrong? Don't you like being my boyfriend?"

"Not particularly."

Chapter Two

Janet and Wiley lived in a high-rise condominium in Arlington, the first suburb across the Potomac into Virginia. They were in the Ballston area, two blocks from a stop on Washington's gradually opening subway system.

They had bought their place after Wiley finished law school. The Ballston subway stop hadn't opened yet, and Wiley knew that as soon as it did, property values would go up by the minute. Arlington was already one of the nation's five wealthiest counties, and the condominium was, to his mind, an investment that they couldn't pass up.

Janet had wanted a house; she was willing to live out in Gaithersburg or Burke if her front door opened to the outside, if she could have a garden out back. But at the time Janet was also losing another disagreement with Wiley, and compared to that, where they lived almost didn't matter. So she had agreed, making him promise that they would move when the subway opened.

But the subway had opened several years ago and they were still there. Ballston was not a pretty place or even a pleasant one, but it was convenient. They could walk to a Y, to the library, to a twenty-four hour Giant grocery store. And the subway made their commutes nearly painless. With both of them working so hard, convenience seemed more important than anything else.

As Wiley held open the glass door of the mauve-and-taupe lobby of their building, Janet spoke over her shoulder. "If you get the mail, I'll go downstairs and get the laundry." The basement level of their building had a few shops, including a dry cleaners. She took all their laundry there, everything except the sheets and towels.

So Wiley was by himself when he unlocked the door of their eleventh-floor corner apartment. He put down his attaché case, hung up his camel coat, and crossed the foyer into the living room. The room was quiet and dark. The two blue-gray love seats faced each other across the low rosewood table.

It was rare that he was here alone like this. Generally Janet was here when he came home. That was one of the things that he had thought of most when he had first decided to ask her to live with him: that she would be home when he got there, that the lights would be on, that dinner would be made, that his home would feel like a home if Janet were in it.

When had everything changed?

The curtains, for instance—they were shut. When they were first married, living on the first floor of a town house over in Adams Morgan, it was an automatic part of Janet's routine to open the curtains in their bedroom and living room each morning and then close them each evening as the sun was setting. She didn't do that any-more. The floor-length drapes, patterned in a quiet Williamsburg blue, were always closed.

And flowers. Once Janet had always had fresh flowers around, on the dining-room table, on the rosewood end tables in the living room, perhaps, but always in the kitchen. Next to the sink, there had been a small vase with at least a sprig or so. "If I've got to cook in a kitchen that doesn't have a window, at least there'll be flowers in it," she had often said.

But now there were no flowers there or any-where, just a scarlet bouquet of silk roses ar-ranged in a silver bowl that Michael Champion had given Janet for Christmas one year.

Michael...

Just how much had changed?

He heard Janet's key in the lock and went out to the foyer to take the dry cleaning from her. He took it into the bedroom and when he came back out, she was in the kitchen, peering into the freezer part of the side-by-side refrigerator. She hadn't taken off her suit jacket.

"Lamb chops or steak?"

Neither sounded right. He'd had a late lunch. "I don't care."

He watched as Janet took out the lamb chops and put them in the microwave to defrost. She also pulled out little foil-wrapped packages that he knew to be twice-baked potatoes. She bought them from a caterer.

The freezer was full of such things. Veal and deboned chicken breasts. Boxes of raspberries, bags of blueberries. Spaghetti sauce and unbaked stomboli that Janet bought at their favorite Italian restaurant. Croissants and bagels from a local bakery. Hors d'oeuvres from a place in New York. Boxes and boxes of Girl Scout cookies. Convenient, expensive, and, except for the Girl Scout cookies, reasonably good.

"Don't we have anything fresh?"

Janet was sprinkling dried rosemary on the lamb chops. "When we only have dinner here once every blue moon, you can't expect anything fresh."

No, he supposed she was right.

Wiley offered to help with dinner. She refused and he started opening the bills that he had put on the counter. They did spend a lot of money. Not just on their food, but on their linens, their glassware, their clothes, everything; they never stopped for bargains anymore. They didn't have time.

But why shouldn't they spend money? Heaven knows they made enough. It only made sense to pay someone else to clean their home; it only made sense to take their laundry out to the most convenient place, to go to stores that would have the clothes they wanted. Anyone with Janet's income shouldn't be sorting through the discount racks at Loehmann's and Mandy's, and Janet didn't do it anymore.

Janet glanced over at him. "Anything interesting in the mail?"

He shook his head. "*The New Yorker* came."

"Isn't this the week for the movies?" Janet only read the Current Cinema column that appeared every other week. The rest of *The New Yorker* didn't really interest her.

He flipped it open, looking at the table of contents. "Yes."

She brought the magazine to the table with her. Clearly she planned to read it during dinner. Well, why not? They didn't have much to say to each other.

Surely it hadn't always been like this. But what did they used to talk about? He couldn't remember.

"What do you plan to do tonight?" he asked.

"I've got some work to do. I was in a meeting all morning and then spent the afternoon returning the phone calls I had gotten during the meeting. I did not write a single word. I sometimes think I do nothing but take phone calls and go to meetings."

She looked up as she spoke, and the light from the brass chandelier shone on the honey-colored warmth of her throat and glittered against the emerald she wore. He had given her that pendant when she had turned thirty last fall.

"I guess I'll start our taxes tonight," he said. They did have that in common; they filed a joint return.

"It's only February."

"I know, but who knows when I'll get another chance."

Janet nodded and turned a page. She was utterly uninterested in financial affairs. That was one thing he had envied Tim Keane for. His wife, Mary, did share at least this interest. They would plan investments together, searching for companies that seemed likely candidates for takeovers. It would be nice to have something like that with Janet. But she cared just as much for the stock market quotations as he did for seed catalogs.

On the other hand, Janet and her movie review were still on the other side of his table. Tim was eating alone tonight.

Janet was sitting sideways on the love seat, her feet tucked beneath her, a yellow legal pad on her lap and three extra number-one pencils on the coffee table. The pad was covered with pencil scratchings. But none of the scratchings had the first thing to do with a new interest rate at a local savings and loan. Janet had been drawing little circles inside big squares.

She was not working. She wasn't even close to working. She was stewing.

Wiley had been angry about dinner, she knew that. Well, not angry. Wiley was careful about what he got angry about. He had been impatient, irritated, disappointed. He had wanted something fresh, something different, for dinner. You could hardly blame him for that.

Of course, she should have gone to the grocery store. Her husband had come home last night after ten days away; the least she could have done was go to the store and buy him an apple and some green beans.

She had meant to go. She had been thinking about it for five days. *Today you will go to the grocery store.* But she kept putting it off. She didn't mind grocery shopping, she never had, so she couldn't figure out why she was so reluctant to go now. But, whatever the reason, she certainly hadn't gone.

Janet had sworn to herself that she would go after work today, but just after five, Alan had come into her office, suggesting that they take their two new clients out for a drink.

"I can't. I have to run some personal errands."

"Personal errands?" Alan ran a hand through his curly dark hair and looked suspicious. No one at the agency was ever discreet about anything. They had no secrets from one another. "Are you going to the doctor? Do you have cancer or something? Are you getting an abortion?"

Alan made a joke about everything.

"Not quite. I am going to the grocery store."

"The grocery store? I thought you never ate at home."

Alan was right. With Wiley gone so much, Janet had gotten into a reasonably regular routine about food. Yogurt and tea in the morning, a decent restaurant lunch with protein, vegetables, and a salad, and an orange and cottage cheese for supper. It wasn't fun, but not eating much at night was the best way for her to control her weight, and she could buy the yogurt, cottage cheese, and oranges from a convenience store on her way home from the subway.

"I might not eat at home," she told Alan, "but my husband does. Or at least he will."

"Your husband? Wiley? Eat at home? Janet, my dear, I had no idea."

He had a point. Wiley had hardly been home at all in the last ten months. "You make it sound like eating at home is a disease."

"At my place it certainly is," Alan responded. "Or at least disease might well be the result."

Michael Champion came into Janet's office. "Disease? Who has a disease?"

"Wiley," Alan answered. "Or at least he's about to get one. Janet's thinking of cooking dinner for him tonight."

"Don't do anything rash," Michael counseled. "My ex made dinner for me once and look what happened to us."

"I'm just going to the grocery store to buy some lettuce."

"Produce is awful at this time of year." Alan took her coat off the hook on the back of the door and waved it at her invitingly. "Why bother?"

"And this is business," Michael added. Michael was always more serious than Alan—not that that was particularly difficult.

"That's right," Alan agreed. "Think how guilty you'll feel when you're lolling around the supermarket while Michael and I must listen to these lawyer-creeps."

Janet laughed. "It's going to do tons of good to have a drink with them if you tell them that you think they are creeps."

"I don't think they are creeps," Michael announced. "Do you know how much money they have?" He took her coat from Alan and held it out for her.

But as they walked to the bar where they were meeting their clients, Janet started to wish that she hadn't let them talk her into this. She had planned on serving fish for dinner. They almost never had fish; she didn't think it froze very well. So whenever she went to the store, they would have fish that night, and then not have it again until—

"Look," Michael interrupted her thoughts, "if you feel guilty, then go ahead and get your groceries."

Janet looked up at him. He was smiling at her, understanding.

That was one thing about the three of them having worked together so closely for so long. They all understood and forgave each other their little weirdnesses. Alan liked to think of himself as eccentric, Michael was obsessively neat, and Janet felt guilty about the strangest things.

That she worked herself into a fit about something as little as grocery shopping surprised no one.

"Sure I feel guilty," she acknowledged, "but Wiley wouldn't skip a drink with a client to do something for me."

Alan laughed. "That sounds more like anger than guilt to me."

"I think I am entitled to be angry," she replied. "Why should I suddenly start being a great wife when he hasn't exactly been a great husband?"

Janet was speaking lightly, but she meant what she was saying. Her life with Wiley had been empty enough before the U.S. Oil case, and this last year had been a complete joke. Wiley had been in Houston all week every week, and there had been many, many Friday afternoons when he'd call at three and say he wasn't going to make it home for the weekend either. He wasn't around for Thanksgiving and had reneged on his promise to come to Mint City for Christmas, leaving her entire hometown to think that her marriage was falling apart.

Maybe her entire hometown was right. She wondered if Wiley could tell the difference between anger and guilt in her voice. Or if he even cared.

"Do you know what?" Alan turned to Michael so calmly that Janet assumed they had gone back to discussing business. "I think Janet's having an affair."

She blinked. What joke file had Alan pulled that one from? "I am not."

"Yes, you are," Alan countered. "Or at least your equivalent of an affair."

"My equivalent?" Janet had no idea what he was talking about.

Michael apparently did. "When other women feel like this," he explained, "they have affairs. You are too much of a wimp to pull that off, so instead you skip buying lettuce. It's entirely in character."

"Well, no wonder I feel guilty." Janet threw up her hands as if the Holy Ghost had just sent her a revelation or two. "Here I thought I was just putting off going to the store; it turns out I am having an affair."

"Is it fun?" Alan asked.

"Don't get pregnant," Michael advised.

Janet laughed, but as they were approaching the bar she grew serious.

They were right. Of course they were; they knew her so well, they knew that there was more involved in her boycott of grocery stores than just laziness.

She had told the two of them about Mary Keane's affair. She hadn't mentioned Mary's name, but Janet had been so shocked when Mary had first told her that she had had to talk to someone. Wiley had been out of town, so she had told Michael and Alan.

But her shock over Mary's affair had faded quickly. She didn't approve of what Mary was doing, but she understood. Mary had wanted to lash out at Tim, to punish him, to make him as miserable as she had been.

And that was how Janet felt about Wiley. She had been lonely, unhappy, angry, and she wanted to punish him for making her feel that way. Only she wasn't capable of having an affair, so she was coming as close as she could.

"It's a pretty sorry excuse for a rebellion," Alan told her.

"But," Michael pointed out, "not going to the grocery store doesn't take up much time. Affairs take too much time. You can't have an affair, Janet, at least not until you get the creative done on all these new accounts. If you need to screw up your marriage, please find some less time-consuming way to do it."

By ten o'clock Janet had switched to drawing little squares inside big circles. She didn't think that the savings and loan would think that a lot of progress toward their new print campaign so she set the pad down on the coffee table and got up.

As usual, she turned off the lights in the living room, put the chain on the door, checked things in the kitchen, and started down the hall toward the bedroom. She had just passed the study when the light under the door reminded her that Wiley was home.

It was strange to have him here.

She rapped lightly on the door and put her head in. "I'm going to bed now."

He was working at the desk. Manila files of receipts and tax forms were open in front of him. He looked up as she spoke.

He had rolled up the sleeves to his white business shirt. His forearms were a warm, rich color and as he leaned back in the chair to look at her, the golden-brown hair on his arms and at the open neck of his shirt glistened in the light from the desk lamp.

"You look good with a tan," she said.

She meant it. It was as if a suntan testified to there being more to Wiley than just the perfect Hastings & Clark associate. She hadn't seen that other side of him in so long that it was nice to have at least this meager reminder.

"Are you very tired?" he asked. If her compliment mattered to him, he didn't say anything. "Or can you answer a few questions about these?" He reached forward and tapped the papers in front of him.

"Fire away."

"This check to Waldenbooks." He picked it up. "You wrote 'deductible' down in the corner. What was it for?"

Janet looked at the check. It was dated last

March. That was eleven months ago. "I haven't a clue," she answered honestly.

"Janet!"

"Well, it was probably for a book." Janet was much better about keeping receipts than she had been when they were first married, but she was still not perfect. "It was either about advertising or something to do with one of our clients."

"I could have guessed that."

Janet felt defensive. "Well, don't you believe me?" At work when she or Alan made a hash of their expense account records—and Alan did it a lot more than she did—Michael took their word— or their guesses—for how much they had spent. If Michael believed her, why didn't Wiley? "I'm very careful about it. When I'm buying a mystery or just a book to read for fun, I pay cash or charge it. Business things I write checks for. I really do."

"I believe you," Wiley answered. "But that's not the point. It's the IRS that you have to convince."

She grimaced. "Anything else?"

"I suppose not." Clearly he had given up expecting explanations from her.

"Then I'm going to bed."

He glanced at his watch. "I'll be in in a minute."

He came into the bedroom just as she was trying to scrape a spot off her skirt with her fingernail. She abandoned the effort, tossed the skirt into the wicker laundry hamper, and finished getting ready for bed. Wiley watched her without saying anything.

As she was turning down the blankets on her side of their king-size bed, he spoke.

"You and Michael Champion seem quite good friends."

She glanced over at him. What a strange thing to say. "That's hardly earth-shattering news. Michael and Alan and I have been friends for years."

"Not you, Alan, and Michael. Just you and Michael."

"What?" She didn't understand.

He shrugged and started to unbutton his shirt. "Never mind."

She didn't like it when he said half of something and then shrugged and said "never mind." It didn't seem fair. "What's this all about? Me and Michael? Of course, we're friends; we've been—"

Oh.

She understood. It wasn't friendship he was talking about. "Are you asking me if I'm having an affair with him?"

Wiley turned away without answering.

"Well, believe what you like." She could hear how flat her voice was. "But it's not true."

He pulled off his shirt, not looking at her. "I would never ask you anything like that."

Janet jerked at the blankets on her side of the bed. Her? An affair? What was wrong with him? She would never have an affair and he had to know it. She might think about one, she might fantasize about some man, but she would never go through with anything. Alan and Michael knew that, they had just been saying so this afternoon. If they knew it, why didn't Wiley?

But he had been asking...asking if she was having an affair with Michael... *Michael?*

How crazy could a person be?

Or how ignorant?

At midnight, Wiley got back up. He couldn't sleep. He didn't know why he had even tried. It was crazy to go to bed at the same time Janet did. She went to sleep so blessed early.

That she went to bed early, that she needed eight hours of sleep every night, while he could do perfectly well on five or six, simply did wonders for their sex life. Either he went to bed with her and then woke up at three in the morning, ready for the day to start, or he came to bed at some reasonable hour and woke her up.

He didn't like waking her up. Of course, there were all the usual nice, generous reasons about not liking to disrupt her sleep, but he was honest enough to admit that it was more than that. Her first groggy, sleep-befuddled reaction was always negative; she would flinch and mumble just as if he were some irritating insect. Even if she was warm and eager moments later, the taste of that initial rejection always lingered.

If only sometimes she would wake him up...

He supposed other couples were direct about this. "You want to have sex?" one would ask. "Sure, why not?" the other would respond.

But he and Janet weren't like that. At least Janet wasn't. If she wanted to make love, she propped herself up on her elbow and started chattering about her day, the weather, anything, until he would laugh and take her in his arms. He suspected that she wasn't even conscious that this was a signal. If asked, she would have just said that she wasn't tired, that that was why she was talking.

But it irritated him sometimes that she couldn't be more direct. He didn't really understand why she couldn't.

He supposed that it was natural that after eight years of marriage their sex life had started to seem a little routine. Like this evening. When he had been watching her undress, he had not felt a thing even though she had been wearing her...well, he wasn't sure what they were called—camisoles, chemises, something like that. They were the top half of a slip.

She had first gotten one a few years ago after buying a blouse that was a great deal sheerer than anything she had ever worn. After one look at herself in the new blouse, she had started to unbutton it. "This goes back to the store."

"I like it," he had said.

"You do?" She faced the mirror again. "But you can see straight through it."

"So?"

She looked at him as if she thought he were about to start molesting small children, but she had kept the blouse and had gotten one of the whatevers to wear underneath it.

The first time she had worn it, she'd clearly felt uncomfortable. Janet was not exactly the world's most provocative dresser.

She was frowning at herself in the mirror. "Does this look all right?"

It looked terrific. "But your bra straps show."

The whatever's shoulder straps were just narrow satin ribbons.

"Well, that's certainly better than the whole bra and most of me showing."

"Take your bra off." And when she started to shake her head automatically, he had continued almost impatiently. "Janet, it's not going to kill you to go without a bra for one night. After all, this is a party, and you'll be with me. No one's going to think you are on the prowl."

So she had, and later that night, when they were dancing in a dark and crowded room, he had flipped open the lapels of his suit jacket before he had pulled her to him. And when he felt her shirt move against his, it was unfamiliar, exciting, not at all married.

Later still at home, as he slid her blouse over her shoulders, he had wanted her to leave this new wisp of satin and lace on. He wanted her beneath him, in nothing but this, this garment whose lace-edged hem brushed against the top of her hips. But when she had started to pull it off, he had not stopped her. Janet was not adventuresome, and Wiley tried hard not to pressure her into doing things she didn't want to.

Still, for months after, the sight of Janet in her camisole had a deliciously forbidden lure.

But that was then. This evening he had watched her idly, watching her undress without any stir of interest.

She was tired. Her body was weary, her movements slow. He felt nothing. She looked so limp, so exhausted, that he couldn't imagine making love to her even if he had wanted to, which he did not.

Wiley went to the rosewood cabinet where they kept their liquor and poured himself some Scotch, then went into the kitchen for ice and water. He got his attaché case out of the foyer and then settled on one of the love seats, his feet propped up on the rosewood table, and tried to work.

... by precluding the defendants from presenting such evidence....

It was funny about marriage. He'd always thought that you got married and then that was it. You didn't have to think about it or worry about it after that. Your career, yes, that had to be worried about, and children and estate planning, all that. But not things with your wife. They were all settled.

But Dan and Tim were worrying. And Wiley was starting to wonder if maybe he should too.

But, no, of course not. How could there be anything wrong with him and Janet? There just couldn't be.

He had been wrong to mention Michael Champion. Wiley didn't know why he had done it; he had thought he had forgotten all about it. He did not, for one minute, believe that Janet was having an affair, he truly did not.

Her reaction had surprised him. He would have expected her to be beside herself, shocked, horrified, frantically examining her own behavior, searching through her memory, hunting for anything she might have said or done to make anyone think this about her.

But her voice had been flat. *Believe what you like, but it's not true.*

Maybe she knew that he didn't believe it;

maybe that was why she sounded so matter-of-fact. Or maybe she just didn't care.

How had they gotten to this point? It was so different back when they were first married, when there had been flowers in the kitchen and fresh vegetables for dinner, when Janet hadn't needed cologne to smell of warmth and vanilla, back when she had still been like she had been when he first met her . . . .

Chapter Three

The year they had met had been an odd one for him, that first year of law school, and Wiley supposed now that if he had met Janet at any other time, he probably wouldn't have fallen in love with her. Loving her had been a product of the moment, a result of what had happened to him the summer before. He had needed her that autumn. Perhaps a year before or a year later, he wouldn't have and then everything would have been entirely different.

Having grown up in New York City, Wiley had, like his father, gone to college at Yale and there wasn't any question that he would, also like his father, go to law school afterward. With his LSAT scores and undergraduate record, he could go anywhere he wanted; it was mostly a matter of whether he wanted to stay in New Haven or go up to Cambridge. At twenty-one, his life was proceeding exactly according to schedule. He was at the right school with the right friends; he was seeing the right women, loving them precisely the right amount.

But then his mother had gotten sick. Cancer. a year, they said, perhaps two.

Wiley had no brothers or sisters; he was his mother's only child. She had no one but his father and him.

His father was in Washington at the time, serving a term on the Securities and Exchange Commission. Wiley assumed that his mother's illness would bring them back to New York. He'd go to Columbia, he thought. That way he could be near her, getting just as good an education as at Harvard or Yale. Columbia wasn't one of the two best law schools in the country, but it was in the top ten. Going to Columbia wouldn't be much of a sacrifice.

But his parents said nothing about coming home, and Wiley decided to apply to Georgetown Law School in Washington.

Georgetown was a very good law school. But Wiley Hunt was not used to the "very good"; he was used to excellence. Georgetown Law felt like a sacrifice, but he was prepared to make it.

The application deadline had passed, and he wondered if he would be turned down for that reason. Deciding that being with his mother while she was sick was more important than his pride, he did what he had never done before, what he had sworn he would never do—he asked his father to pull some strings.

His father almost refused. "Georgetown! Wiley, why?"

"To be with Mother."

"But she doesn't expect you to. This is your career, your future. This could be a serious setback. She wouldn't want you to."

"I want to."

"If we were home, then Columbia...."

"But we aren't home. Would you call?"

The phone call probably wasn't necessary, but Wiley D. Hunt made it, and when Wiley L. told his mother he would be in Washington with her, it was the first time he had ever seen her cry.

He didn't work that summer and spent all of his time with her, whether she was in the hospital or in the house they had rented in Northwest D.C. It was more time that he had ever spent with her before. Even in the summers of his childhood when she had taken him to their cottage in Maine, with his father visiting them on weekends, Wiley had not spent as much time with her as he was now.

She told him about his grandparents, about her own childhood. She had him write down things, a few of her favorite recipes that she hoped someday someone would want to make for him. She told him about her jewelry, when his father had given her each piece. "The earrings, the diamond ones, he gave me when you were born. When you get married, you should give them to your wife. And these opals . . . I wore them to our wedding; if you marry a girl with an October birthday, maybe she'd like to wear them too. Opals are supposed to be bad luck if they aren't your birthstone."

Wiley explained the rules of soccer to her, and he read aloud to her, at last growing to understand why Robert Browning had always been her favorite poet. As she was dying, mother and son became friends.

She deteriorated more rapidly than expected, and in early September she died. And Wiley was so incapable of expressing his grief that he could only be angry that now he was stuck at George-town Law.

In October the Foreign Service family who owned the house the Hunts had been living in were suddenly transferred back to Washington. The lease gave them rights to have the house back. The two Wileys, a grim and silent pair, were happy to let it go.

The younger Wiley moved into a house quite typical of many young D.C. residents. It was a group house, a collection of people living under one roof, sharing rent and expenses, and in some cases, meals and friendship, trying to construct some sort of family out of what drifted in on the waves of want ads and bulletin board notices.

There were seven people in this house; some were law students, some had jobs. One of the latter was Janet Barnum, a case worker for a Midwestern congressman.

At first Wiley simply regarded her as an anthropological exhibit, an artifact from a foreign culture. Small, pretty, and brown-haired, she seemed to conform to every stereotype of Midwesterners that he had had. She was lively and open, even-tempered and relentlessly cheerful; her feelings were easily stirred. She could bake, not just cakes and banana bread, but pie crust and yeast dough. "You just have to show the yeast who's boss," she said, laughing. For someone who worked for a congressman, she seemed to have no political interests, and Wiley soon labeled her as being without depth or complexity, a feeling that seemed confirmed because she never ate a sandwich without white bread and mayonnaise.

He happened to come into the kitchen one evening as she was making dinner. She was taking a bunch of broccoli out of the refrigerator.

"You're just in time," she said, "to stop me from overcooking the vegetables."

"I beg your pardon?"

"Oh, that's right. You were off studying. Well, you missed a major family discussion about how Janet always overcooks the vegetables."

Vegetables. His mother's vegetables had always been lightly steamed, the textures crisp, the colors brilliant.

"People can cook as they like when it is their turn," he said diplomatically.

"That's right." She laughed. "And when it's my turn, those vegetables are going to be boiled into submission. That's how we cook where I come from."

She untwisted the wire that held the broccoli together and began to pull the leaves off.

"Where are you from?" he asked.

"You've asked me that three times."

"I have?" He was surprised; he didn't remember. "Have you answered?"

"Mint City, Missouri, every time."

Mint City meant nothing to him, and Missouri only a little more. "I'm sorry," he apologized, conscious of how insulting it was that he had forgotten. He had probably only asked to be polite. "I suppose it's that I don't have a very clear grip on the difference between the states out there and they all blur together."

"That's okay."

"Did you go to the University of Missouri?" He searched his memory. "Isn't it in Columbia?"

"Yes, it's in Columbia, and yes, I went there."

"Did you graduate last spring?"

She shook her head. "Actually, this is my senior year. I've done all my course work; I've just got to write my senior paper this year."

"Why are you here?" He was now more curious than polite.

She explained how her congressman knew her father, how he liked to bring staff in from his district.

That wasn't an answer. "But I thought all nice Midwestern girls spent their senior year of college planning their weddings."

"Perhaps you don't know as much about 'nice Midwestern girls' as you think you do."

"I don't know a thing," he admitted promptly. "You're the first one I've ever met.... You are one, aren't you? A nice Midwestern girl, I mean."

"More or less." And through this whole conversation she had never stopped working on dinner.

As in many group houses, the various household chores—cooking, shopping, dishes, cleaning—were governed by an elaborate chart that rotated the different tasks among the seven of them. After dinner that night, Janet stood up. "Lick your plates, please. I'm on dishes."

"But didn't you make dinner?" Wiley asked. Of course she had, he'd been standing right there while she'd done it.

She shrugged and smiled, saying nothing, starting to gather up the plates.

"Wait a minute," he continued. "You shouldn't be on dinner and dishes the same day."

"What difference does it make?"

He picked up several plates and followed her into the kitchen. He checked the schedule, written out on a sheet of yellow legal paper and magneted to the refrigerator. Janet was on dishes tonight, but someone else had been on dinner.

"Did you trade with Glenn? Why isn't he in here?"

She started to fill the sink with water. "He must have forgotten about dinner. I was here; I wasn't doing anything."

The light in the kitchen was a soft yellow, and the room was warm. White bubbles frothed in the sink and Janet started to put the glasses in, slipping them in sideways. They filled with suds and sank.

"Why do you let people take advantage of you like that?"

She didn't stop working. "What difference does it make?"

"It's not fair."

"Maybe not, but don't you think it's a waste of time to worry about what's fair all the time? The world's not going to come to an end because I'm doing dinner and dishes."

"Presumably I wouldn't be in law school if I didn't think fairness rather important."

Suddenly she smiled, her brown eyes sparkling. "Now, don't tell me you are confusing what is legal with what is fair. If so, you better go study some more. You've got a lot more to learn about the law."

But he didn't. Instead he picked up a towel and started drying glasses for her.

After that, Wiley started watching more carefully. He hadn't noticed before, but she did more than her share around the house. A lot more. Not just doing jobs that weren't on her schedule, but she did all the little things as well. Picking up coffee cups from the living room, folding up the newspapers, sorting the mail, putting away records. The house was a clean, comfortable place because of Janet.

At the monthly house meeting in December he brought it up. "We're letting Janet pick up too much of the slack."

No one denied it, and Wiley wondered if he had been the last to notice. She did have a funny look on her face, and he could see why. A few weeks ago he could hardly remember her name; now he was acting like her champion.

"This is not worth talking about," she said emphatically.

"No, I think we are all taking advantage of you."

Of course, everyone agreed with him, and all resolved to do better...but when the meeting broke up, it was Janet who started picking up the beer cans and coffee cups.

Once again he followed her into the kitchen.

"What brought that on?" she asked.

"Just the way things are."

"I didn't think you noticed what happened around here."

"I do live here." He felt a little defensive.

"Well, you may live here, but you don't study

here, and that's what you do all the time. It's not healthy.''

She was right. He was studying very hard, harder than he ever had in college. He knew exactly what he was doing. He was working for grades. Sometimes he sacrificed knowledge for grades; if something wasn't going to be on the exam, he didn't learn it, no matter how interesting it was.

And he knew why he was going for grades—it was to make up for not being at Harvard or Yale. He had to graduate at the top of his class to compensate for the Georgetown diploma. If he were at one of the very best schools, his class rank wouldn't matter so much; he wouldn't have felt this pressure.

That Christmas was the worst of Wiley's life. The house emptied out; everyone had a home to go to, but he and his father were not going back to New York. Although neither was willing to admit to such emotionalism, they just couldn't face their New York brownstone, not without the woman who'd been wife to one and mother of another. So they both worked steadily throughout the holidays and then ate Christmas dinner in a restaurant, talking of contract law during the festivities.

Wiley's other housemates began drifting back to Washington before New Year's, but it wasn't until Janet came back from Missouri—or Miz-ur-ah, as she pronounced it—that Wiley felt like things were back to normal.

She turned up on a snowy afternoon. He had been studying in his bedroom, and from the window, he saw her step out of a taxi. Unthinkingly he dropped his pen and hurried downstairs.

He got to the door as she did, opening it for her. She looked healthy and rested. There was a fresh dusting of freckles across her cheeks, and a few melting snowflakes glittered in the satin of her hair. He reached for her, but, at the last moment, checked himself and took her luggage instead. "Why didn't you let me know when you were coming in? I would have come to the airport for you."

She blinked and stared. And Wiley cursed himself. Why had he said that? Of course she was surprised. He had never before said or done a thing to suggest that he was willing to do such favors for her.

But now he was willing. Very willing. He just hadn't known it before.

Chapter Four

Wiley had no idea how to conduct a romance with a housemate. He could not date Janet in the usual sort of way. Not only did it seem very odd for him to take her out to dinner when they ate together every night anyway, but anything like that would be so public, everyone in the house would know. By the time they'd get back from dinner, the rest of the house would have probably rented out Janet's room, assuming that she wouldn't need it anymore. There would be no room for the leisurely beginnings, for the slow decidings.

So he did nothing, but when he was in the house, he watched her, listened to her, learned about her.

Wiley learned that there had indeed been someone back in Missouri with whom Janet was to have planned a wedding. She had been dating him since before she could walk, she said. But the unofficial engagement had been broken, and that was, in truth, why she had come to Washington.

She had told this story at dinner one evening, speaking of it in the most casual way, but he followed her into the kitchen before remarking.

"I'm sorry," he said quietly. "About your broken engagement, that is."

"Don't be. He and I were too much alike. It was easy but we were probably pretty boring. I'm glad we found out."

"How did you find out?"

"*I* didn't. He did. He met someone else."

Wiley winced. "That must have been rough."

"Well, yes. I went around feeling defective for a while, like a bit of a sexual reject, but I'm pretty tough. I think I'm over it."

It seemed odd, Janet calling herself tough. He wouldn't have thought it; she seemed so emotional. She cried more easily than anyone he had ever met, not knock-down, screaming, shrieking hysterics, of course, just a few quick tears over the littlest things—news shows about a man giving a kidney to his young daughter or tapes of Olympic gold medalists listening to "The Star-Spangled Banner." Anyone capable of crying over "The Star-Spangled Banner" did not deserve to be thought of.

But think of her he did, and one Sunday afternoon in late January, when their other housemates all had dinner plans, he suggested they go to a restaurant together. Wiley made the invitation sound much more casual than it really was.

"Do you want to come in for a nightcap?" Janet asked as they approached the front door afterward.

"I don't think so," he replied. "I need to be getting on home; it's such a long drive."

"Well, do drive carefully," she said as he held open the door for her.

The house was quiet. Either people were still out, or they had gone to bed. The reading lamp by the side of the sofa was the only light still on downstairs.

It was an awkward moment. They were both standing by the stairs. Wiley wasn't sure what to do.

She glanced at her watch. "Goodness, it's almost one. I had no idea it was so late. I thought it was only eleven."

She must have had a good time; he was glad. "I thought you turned into a pumpkin at midnight."

Janet's little laugh was constrained, self-conscious. She went into the living room, switched off the lamp, then came back to the stairs. "Well... thanks for dinner."

"My pleasure."

A faint light came down from the upstairs hall. Her blouse was cream with faint stripes of bittersweet and moss green.

It was intriguing that beneath this apple-clean, Girl Scout appearance was a woman whose eyes had gone dark when she looked at him, a woman whose breath came in soft gasps.

"Well..." Again she was hesitant. "I guess if I am going to turn into a pumpkin, I should do it in the privacy of my own bedroom."

She started up the stairs.

"No." He took her arm, stopping her. "This is something I'd like to watch."

Once, years later, Wiley wondered if he had not made some very serious mistakes that night.

Janet was not a virgin, but she might as well

have been. Her encounters with the Missouri boy-friend had given her neither technique nor experience.

Of course, Wiley had doubts of his own, questions about his performance, his ability to please her—what man didn't think about such matters when he was with a particular woman for the first time?

But in the face of Janet's uncertainties, he repressed his own, wanting to appear completely confident, completely in control. His manner allowed, perhaps encouraged, her to be passive. She had to initiate nothing. He undressed himself, he guided her hand to his body, he expected nothing of her but that she follow his lead.

And that first night seemed to have set a pattern that had persisted even through eight years of marriage.

Just as expected, Wiley and Janet immediately became a very settled thing in the house. They were treated as a couple, referred to as a unit, expected to speak with one voice. It was intimacy without isolation, emphasizing their similarities, obscuring their differences.

And in early spring Wiley told Janet that he loved her.

Easter that year was everything that Christmas was not. The law school had a break and Congress was on recess, so everyone in the house would be leaving as they had at Christmas—except Janet was not going.

"It will be the first holiday I've missed," she said a little glumly. "But Nancy"—Nancy was her older sister—"will be coming out next week, so at least I'll see her."

"Can I be selfish and say that I'm glad you will be here?"

Those days they had together with just the two of them living in the house were, for Wiley, everything he had missed since first learning that his mother was dying. Janet wasn't maternal; she didn't mother him—at least not much—but her presence was a domestic one, quiet, settled, reassuring. He felt like he had a home again—he and his father were still avoiding New York—and he knew that this house felt like a home, not because it was where he was living, but because it was where Janet was living.

On the night before Easter, he tried to tell her. "This is nice, you and I, alone together."

"Well, sure," she said, "you just like being waited on."

"It's a little more than that. It's nice not to have to trample over five other people when I want to get to you."

"That's what I mean. You're lazy."

"Janet, be serious. What do you say, when the lease is up in June, that you and I get a place of our own?"

She stared at him. "A place of our own? The two of us?"

"Of course, the two of us." And when she didn't say anything, he went on. "Why don't we live together?"

"Live together?"

Why was she so surprised? They loved each other; this being with five other people was hardly perfect. Living together was only logical, wasn't it?

He hadn't expected to have to talk her into it, but he didn't mind. Talking her into it would be fun, especially as he didn't intend to do much talking. He pulled her down on his lap and murmured into her hair.

She struggled free. "No."

He was confused. "No?"

"I can't live with you."

"You don't want to?" She was standing, so he stood too. "This surprises me. I would have hoped you would have wanted this as much as I did."

She was pale, tense, trying not to cry. "Of course I want to. I'd love it, but..."

"But what?"

"I just can't."

"Why not?"

"My parents... it would hurt them so. It was hard enough making them understand about this house, it being co-ed and all, and if I were..."

"I understand." What else could he say? This was how she felt; he had to respect that. "I'm just sorry, that's all."

And he was disappointed. He really did want to have her to himself. He was tired of seeing her pick up after other people. He didn't want to spend another year watching everyone else take advantage of her.

But if her father and mother were old-fashioned enough to be bothered by something like that... well, there was nothing to be done.

Wiley's father was taking them both out to dinner on Easter Sunday. He and Janet had never met.

As soon as they did, Wiley realized that he had not given his father an at all accurate impression of his relationship with Janet. Lee—as the senior Wiley was known to his friends—seemed to think her nothing more than one of Wiley's housemates who happened to be alone on a holiday. So he was pleasant and impersonal without subjecting her to the scrutiny he might have if he had known that his only son had just asked her to live with him.

It was interesting, Wiley found, to listen to Janet answer his father's questions about her work in the congressman's office. Her political notions were far better thought out than he had had any idea. He had assumed that her "help other people at all times" was a habit left over from Girl Scouts, that her "do unto others" was a relic of her Bible Belt Sunday school, that these were ideals easier to practice in the uncomplicated world she had come from. But as she talked with his father, Wiley realized that her moral and social values had a steady pragmatic base—helping other people was a good way to avoid social unrest.

At the end of dinner Lee put his napkin on his plate and spoke to Wiley. "Son, I think we need to do something about clearing up your mother's things."

Wiley froze. His mother's things, her clothes, her jewelry. He did not want to do this. Not at all. "Isn't there . . . haven't any of her friends offered . . ."

"No one has said anything."

Wiley was silent. But he knew he had to do it. As bad as it would be for him, it would be worse for his father. "I'm not really sure I know what to do, but of course I will."

"Thank you," his father said.

There was a pause and then Janet spoke. "I've done things like this before. I'll go up with you if you need help."

Wiley turned to her in relief, silently blessing her. It would be so much easier with her there.

"The weekend after Nancy leaves," she suggested. "Why don't we go up then?"

Nancy Barnum Baker arrived a week later, and Wiley found it a little eerie to be around her. She and Janet didn't look particularly alike, but their mannerisms, their gestures, their patterns of speech, inflection—and sleeping patterns—were so very much the same, that finally he had to remark on it.

"Oh, goodness." Nancy laughed. "You'd go mad if you ever came to Mint City. All three of us girls sound just like Mother, and everybody says she sounds like her sister. We're all the same, from Grandma on down."

The thought of there being five other Janets, spread out over three generations, was unnerving. She seemed so special to him.

Janet took several days off work, and while the sisters did some sight-seeing, mostly they sat home and talked.

"What did you two do all day?" he would ask as he took them out to dinner in the evening.

"Gabbed," one of them would reply.

And then they would both laugh at his expression. It was so clear he couldn't understand how two people could simply chatter away an entire day.

So he wasn't surprised when very early one morning as he went toward the kitchen, he heard their voices.

But what they were saying did surprise him.

"You were right," Nancy was saying. "He is something. Not only does he look as great as you said he did—"

Wiley had this sinking feeling that they were not talking about the Jefferson Monument.

"—but he's so . . . I don't know . . . so urbane. Is that a silly word?"

"It's probably a polite one," Janet replied bluntly.

Nancy laughed. "Well, yes, I've always been a sucker for his type. I was surprised when you said you were sleeping with him—"

Wiley jerked in surprise. What extraordinary things women told one another.

"—but now that I've seen him, I understand it."

Janet spoke. "He's asked me to live with him next year."

"He has? Are you going to?"

Janet must have shaken her head, for Nancy continued. "What did you tell him?"

"That Mother and Daddy would die."

Nancy made a noise. "Now, Janet, you know that's not true. They might mind a little, but they wouldn't die. They'd figure that you had your reasons."

"I know."

What's this? Wiley wondered. She'd said . . .

"Is it that he's not very committed to you?"

"Oh, on a short-term basis he is," Janet answered. "I know he'd never start seeing someone else or anything like that, but he doesn't feel like he's in for the long haul. When we'd run into a serious problem, it would be over."

Nancy seemed to agree. "And I guess your backgrounds are different enough that there'd be problems. And you know what Mother always said, sometimes it's only the promise that keeps two people together during the bad times. But if he were really committed, would you live with him?"

"Presumably then his question would have been different."

"You would marry him, wouldn't you?"

Marry? Wiley gripped the back of a chair. Good God, why were they talking about marriage? Who had said one word about that? Who was thinking about that? *Marriage?*

Janet's voice was clear, cool. "It's hardly relevant. He's not going to ask."

Going up to New York to sort through his mother's things was now even more uncomfortable. From Janet's first glimpse around his parents' brownstone, everything that happened reminded Wiley of the sisters' conversation.

"I knew you were different," Janet said as she walked around the house, "but I had no idea your family had so much money." Her voice had been careful, not really like her own.

"We don't really." He tried to reassure her. "My father makes a lot, of course, but there's not much real family money."

Janet gestured at the dining room, with its deep bay windows and Chippendale chairs. "Where I come from, we call this real money."

Did she think that was it? That that was why he did not plan on marrying her? Because she didn't come from a moneyed background? He hoped she didn't think that, because it wasn't true. Not at all.

"Well, let's get to work," she said.

They started with the clothes, preparing to give them to one of the Junior League shops. Wiley took things out of the garment bags while Janet folded and sorted, telling him what to write on the inventory they would need for his father's tax return.

His mother had had lovely things. She had worn pale colors, oysters and ivories, camels, golds, and rose. Soft, thick wool suits lined with real satin; cocktail dresses, floating chiffon, the older ones having hand-sewn beading, the new ones with hand-painted designs. The labels on the clothes meant nothing to Janet, but clearly she recognized the quality. She sewed; she knew all sorts of strange things about seams and button-holes, and several times he noticed her admiring a detail of the workmanship as she worked, check-ing the pockets, folding the garments.

In the hall closet he found his mother's mink. He brought it back into the bedroom, where Janet was still unhanging blouses.

"What shall we do with this? I don't—"

Janet let a blouse fall to the bed. "Is that mink?" She came near and fingered it, her fingers sinking into the lustrous weight of the almost champagne-colored fur. "I've never felt a mink before."

"Should we just put it in with the other things?" he asked. "I suspect it's very expensive."

"Wiley, I think perhaps you ought to hold on to this."

"Whatever for?"

She turned away, picking up the white silk blouse she had dropped. She didn't look at him. "I've got a beaver jacket of my grandmother's. It's pretty funky, but I really like wearing it because it was hers."

He had seen the jacket. He thought it a nightmare. "I rather doubt that either Dad or I would ever want to wear this."

She smiled, a polite, tight smile. She still didn't look at him. "You'll probably have a daughter someday. So if you can afford to pay storage on it..."

A daughter!

Oh, well, he supposed she was right. Of course he'd marry someday—not now, not soon, but someday. Of course he'd have a child. That's what people did.

"We can afford the storage," he said, his voice as tight as hers.

But how odd. If he married in his early thirties, as his father had done, this coat would not be worn again until sometime in the twenty-first century.

Again and again it came up—this question of his future, a time when he would be settled, when there would be a woman he planned to spend his life with, a woman he would want to have his mother's things. That was the reason why all her jewelry had been left to him—so that he could give it to his wife, his daughter.

And Janet had to know this, she had to be thinking this, as she looked through the jewelry, opening the velvet boxes, seeing what should be sent to the appraiser. Her voice was light, her manner offhand. "Shall we call these pretty blue stones or shall we call them sapphires?"—but if what she and her sister had been saying were true, this had to hurt.

She must feel used, cheap.

But she was as tough as she once said she was. He was astonished at her fortitude. She was so easily stirred by the smallest things that he had dreaded doing this with her. Over and over he had had to fight down the ache that came with his mother's memory, the dull misery of her absence. If Janet had been as weepy or sentimental as he had every reason to expect her to be, it would have been impossible.

But clearly when she had to, Janet could control herself. When they found three letters that his mother's first fiancé had written her before D day, when they found with them the now-empty engagement ring which he had given her, Janet had blinked and swallowed hard.

But when she spoke, her voice was brisk. "I imagine that after he was killed, she gave the diamond back to his family."

Wiley blessed her. If she had cried, he probably would have too.

He wanted to explain. He wanted to tell her why he had asked her to live with him, why he wasn't thinking about marriage, why he wouldn't. He would tell her about the pressures of law school and about what it was like to join a firm, how much work it was. How crazy it was to take on any other obligations. But he didn't know how to bring it up; he didn't know what he would say.

But at last he heard Janet exclaim, "Look, aren't these the opals that we saw?"

She was looking at his parents' wedding picture. Against the satin bodice of his mother's wedding gown was the opal pendant. "Yes, they are. Opals were her birthstone."

"Were they? They're—"

She broke off. But Wiley knew what she was going to say. "They're mine too." She had an October birthday.

Maybe that's what he should do to show her how much he appreciated her help in this, get her an opal, a pendant or earrings. Yes, that's what he would do. He hadn't given her a present yet, and he'd like to. He'd look for something next week.

Janet went on. "When did they get married?"

He suspected that she didn't care, that she was just asking to cover up what she had almost said, but he told her anyway. And then realized that this was his chance.

"My father was thirty-two, I think." He tried to keep his voice casual. "None of my family has ever married early. That's why I've never thought of myself as doing so."

"Wiley, you're almost twenty-three."

"Right."

"Where I come from, that's not marrying early," she said bluntly. "That's *late.*" She put down the picture. "Now, let's tackle these drawers."

Again and again all weekend, Janet impressed him with her stamina, her strength. She had common sense, she could decide what they should keep, what they should discard. Left to their own devices, he and his father would have kept the house a museum or they would have gotten rid of everything. They could not have made the kind of piece-by-piece decisions that Janet was making. And Wiley knew that someday when he wanted his mother's mementos, he would have Janet to thank for preserving them.

And even more important than how well she was doing this was the fact that she was doing this at all. No one else had offered. She was doing more than her share. But Janet always did more than her share.

It was easy to underestimate Midwesterners. But you had to remember the pioneer stock that they sprang from. Their ancestors, the early settlers, had had to be generous; a family never knew when disaster would strike them, when they would need help themselves. And they had to be tough. Maybe they could let themselves cry over the little things as Janet did. But they couldn't cry over the big ones; there were just too many of them.

And when Wiley went to a jewelry store to look at opals, he heard himself ask the jeweler to show him the diamonds.

Wiley rather dreaded telling his father that he was marrying Janet. He wasn't sure why, and he tried to tell himself that it was just that he didn't like pulling surprises, and this would certainly be a surprise.

Lee Hunt went very still, and it was a moment before he spoke. "That's wonderful news; she seemed like a lovely girl."

What else could he say?

He did allow himself to show surprise that they were getting married in June.

"Well, it's just that the lease on the house is up, and.. " Then Wiley realized what his father was thinking. "No, Dad, she's not pregnant."

He expected Lee to deny even thinking such a thing, but he did not. "I'm glad to hear that. I'd hate to think you were having to marry."

Wiley shook his head. "No, I'd have never let that happen."

"Good." And then Lee paused as if he were deciding whether or not to go on. "I believe I do not interfere in your life unduly, Wiley—"

Wiley nodded in quick agreement.

"—but I would think things would be easier if you put off starting a family."

"Oh, Lord, yes."

And Wiley's voice had been so emphatic that his father had to smile. "Then what do you and I do about the wedding? I have a feeling we're going to miss your mother badly. She'd tell us what we are supposed to do."

"I imagine we need to show up."

"We can probably manage that." Lee then asked how much money the Barnums had, something that Wiley simply did not know. Dick Barnum was a veterinarian with a large animal practice. Neither of the Wileys had much sense of what kind of income this produced.

"Try to see if they need help with putting on the wedding," Lee said. "We don't want to offend, but weddings are expensive. Perhaps I could pay for the liquor at the reception. That would be easy to handle tactfully and it might make things considerably easier for them."

Wiley mentioned this to Janet, saying that his father would like to do something.

Janet stared at him. "Have you lost your mind? Liquor at a wedding? Where did you grow up?"

It turned out that Janet had never been to a wedding where liquor had been served—wedding receptions in her hometown were strictly mints, punch, and cake in the church basement. She had nothing against liquor, and her parents—well, her father—did have an occasional drink, but the Barnums were certainly not going to be the first family in Mint City to stage a wedding with liquor.

Wiley immediately began discouraging his friends from coming. They expected weddings to be a big weekend blowout. From the rehearsal dinner on Friday to the brunch on Sunday, a wedding was to be a continuous party. Such an affair was clearly worth traveling halfway across the country for.

But this would be a neat, tidy ceremony, twenty minutes in the sanctuary, an hour or two in the church social hall, and then Janet would change into her going-away suit and people would throw rice and they would be off. It hardly seemed worth it for even Wiley to go.

But, of course, he went as did his father, and all

went according to schedule. Janet's something
borrowed was her mother's dress, her something
old her grandmother's cameo. Wiley had said
nothing to her about the opals.

It wasn't so bad, being married while in law
school. In fact, Wiley soon concluded, it was a
great deal better than not being married. Janet was
wonderfully understanding. Apparently she and
her sister had grown up hearing their mother joke
about never having seen their father when he had
been in veterinarian school.

The crisis came when law school was over. Interested in regulatory law, Wiley took a job with
Hastings & Clark. "At a New York firm, I'd be
coming down to D.C. all the time anyway. We
might as well live here."

He was glad that his interests had inclined him
to Washington. He knew Janet did not want to
live in New York; she didn't even think it a nice
place to visit. At least they had avoided that problem.

But not the other one.

Janet wanted a baby.

It seemed impossible that they could have so
completely misunderstood each other. Janet had
thought that it went without saying that when law
school was over, she'd quit work and they'd start
their family. After all, that's what her parents had
done.

He too had also assumed that he would do as
his parents had done. He had not been born until
after his father had been made partner. You don't
want a baby during those first grueling years with

a firm. There's too much at stake to have that kind of disruption and responsibility.

Wiley was twenty-five. He still felt young. He never expected to be a husband already, and he couldn't imagine himself as a father.

He had been firm and Janet had yielded. "There's not a lot else I can do," she said unhappily.

Of course, there was a great deal she could have done, since she was the one taking birth control pills, but it obviously never occurred to her to arrange the sort of "accident" that occasionally happened to women whose husbands weren't ready to have children. Janet would never consider doing that, and he guessed that he ought to be grateful.

So when he passed the bar exam, they had moved into the high-rise condominium.

Janet wasn't happy. She was bored with her job, doing casework for a congressman. It hadn't bothered her when she thought that she would be leaving it soon, but now that that moment had been postponed for years, she was restless.

When Michael Champion had wanted her to join his fledgling agency, Wiley had encouraged her.

He had never thought of advertising as a career for her—she hadn't either—but Champion wanted her to write the brochures and leaflets that were the bread and butter of a small agency.

Janet did have the most utterly unselfconscious prose of anyone Wiley had ever encountered. He had always assumed that her writing style came from a certain naiveté, that she just wrote as she talked. Her congressional boss and his constituents had loved her easy, informal style; she would probably do just fine in this new job.

She did more than fine. The agency was small enough that little was set or formal. Ideas were thrown around, and some of the best were Janet's.

She now had nearly the same responsibilities as did Alan, one of the firm's two founders. He was creative director and art director; she was senior writer. He was visual; she was verbal. They worked together extremely well, and they worked extremely hard.

Janet was defensive about her job—at least she was around her husband. She was continually saying that some of the nation's most creative people were in advertising. She claimed that it was art as well as commerce; that the commerce, the need to speak to the hearts of thousands, of millions, gave the art vitality and energy.

Well, all that might be true, but she wrote about foot powder, health insurance, and, on good days, powdered lemonade. Wiley couldn't help thinking that it was less dignified, less important than the law.

He loved everything about his own job. The travel didn't bother him, and the work was so interesting he hardly ever knew where he was. And now that the U.S. Oil case was over, now that it seemed as certain as it could be that he would be made partner, he thought that perhaps he and Janet could start doing some of the things that they had been putting off. Like more vacations. They hadn't taken one together in over two years. He hadn't been away at all, except this trip down to the Caribbean with his father last week, and she had just taken a few extra days when she had been traveling on business, staying on in California by herself or stopping off in Missouri to see her family.

But once he was made partner, they could start taking more time off. They could get the house that Janet had wanted. They could even have a baby, all the things that she had wanted six years ago. She'd be able to have them now. Didn't she know that?

Chapter Five

"I see it as San Francisco," Alan declaimed with a gesture designed, perhaps, to mimic the Golden Gate bridge. "This ad cries 'San Francisco.'"

Janet laughed as she walked toward her office. "I don't know about the ad, Alan, but I talked to the client and he cried, 'do it cheap.' We could never go to California for the shoot; we'd have to buy stock footage, and you know it." She was very used to being the only person in the Creative Division who paid attention to the budget. Alan certainly did not.

"Janet." Her secretary, Kris, waved a handful of pink message slips. "Here are your calls."

Janet didn't take them. "One hour? I got all these calls in one hour?"

"What about Bangkok?" Alan put in. "Shanghai?"

"What about Anacostia?" Janet returned. "I hear it's nice in the spring." Anacostia was the worst part of Washington.

"Will you please take these?" Kris moaned. "My arm's about to drop off." Kris propped her right arm across her typewriter as if the weight of Janet's message slips were too much to bear.

Alan took the messages and followed Janet into her office.

As soon as the door was closed he started trying to tuck them, one by one, into the breast pocket of Janet's blazer.

She waved his hand away. "Now, is that professional, Alan? Trying to cop a feel when you're delivering phone messages?"

"It entirely depends on what profession you're in," he answered cheerfully.

"We're in advertising."

"Since most people think that that's a step below prostitution, then, yes, I should think this is very professional." He slipped another message in her pocket.

"Will you stop that?" She grabbed the rest of the slips from him. "I don't need you sniffing around my chest. Why, just the other day Wiley accused me of having an affair with Michael. I don't need—"

"*What?*"

Janet stopped, startled. "You heard me. Wiley asked if I were involved with Michael."

"An affair? You?"

"I don't think he believes it, but—"

"I should hope not."

Janet was surprised. Alan was almost never serious. *I should hope not.* That was serious. She smiled at him, about to thank him for his support, but he caught her glance and then turned away, almost as if he were embarrassed.

She thought it rather sweet. He did care a lot about her.

But he recovered quickly. "Wiley thinks it's Michael? Why Michael?" he complained. "Why not me?"

This was the usual Alan.

"Why isn't he worried about me?" he continued. "No woman in her right mind would take Michael if she could have me. I'm elegant, I'm gorgeous—"

"You wear Hawaiian shirts."

"Yes," he agreed, "but I am elegant and gorgeous in them."

"The question is what are you like out of them."

"Do you want to see?" Alan instantly loosened his tie and started to unbutton the pale yellow oxford-cloth shirt that Michael forced him to wear.

"No, I don't. I just had lunch."

Alan straightened his tie and ambled out of her office. She overheard him tell Kris in very loud tones that the women around here didn't know what they were missing.

Janet smiled. She was crazy about Alan. He was a little hard to take sometimes—he was pretty self-centered—but the two of them did work very well together. They spent a lot of time in one another's offices, staring into space together, conceiving an ad as a team. She would write a headline or Alan would slash out a sketch; they would tape it on the wall and stare at it mindlessly until one of them thought of something. And they always did. The hard energy of his electric visions and the soft sentimentality of her feelings blended into astonishingly effective ads.

She sat down at her desk and flipped through her messages. They were the usual sort of thing—a couple of people looking for jobs, a film production house wanting to play their demo reel for her, Accounting complaining that Creative had gone over budget on a florist's campaign.

One personal call had come in, from Mary Keane. Normally, Janet would have returned the professional calls first, but Janet hadn't talked to Mary since the other woman had left Tim. Janet dialed Mary's office and sat back in her pale gray chair as Mary's secretary put her on hold.

Janet's office was very high-tech. Her desk and the little round conference table were glass. Her chair and carpeting were an impractical pearl gray and everything else—the credenza, the cabinets, the narrow blinds, the stands for the video tape deck and monitor—was dazzling white. Janet, who had had nothing to do with choosing all this whiteness, thought it was a bit too much like the set for a toothpaste commercial. She was waiting for the day when her office fixtures would come alive, kicking their little chrome legs up in the air and singing about white teeth being happy teeth.

The color in the office came from things that belonged to Janet. Between the windows was an old four-player pinball machine with a back glass featuring a pack of cards rigged out as a late sixties rock band in swirls of turquoise, red, and purple. Hung on the opposite wall were framed labels of antique fruit crates and vegetable tins, Columbia Belle apples, King's Cadet asparagus, and Princess oranges, blushingly healthy produce on backgrounds of royal blue and vermilion. The pinball machine and the fruit labels were the only things in her office that Janet particularly liked.

Maybe that's why she closed her eyes whenever she leaned back in her chair.

She opened them as soon as Mary answered.

"Mary, how are you?"

"Alive. Listen, do you want to have lunch next week?"

Janet pulled her calendar out from under a pile of spiral-bound casting books. "Tuesday or late on Thursday."

"No, not Tuesday and Thursday's bad. What about the week after? Monday?"

"Wednesday?"

"No, that won't work."

"Then it will have to be in three weeks."

"I'm still open that whole week."

"I'm free on—" Janet broke off. This was ridiculous. "Let's not wait that long. What about dinner?"

"Isn't Wiley in town?"

"So?"

Mary paused. "Well, good for you."

They decided to see each other that evening even though Wiley had only returned from the Caribbean a few days before. Janet called to tell him. Of course, she couldn't get through—she didn't expect to be able to; an important client probably could have, but not a wife—so she left a message with his secretary.

Just as she was getting ready to leave that evening, Michael stepped into her office. He frowned at the clutter on her desk, but didn't comment on it. "Do you have a second?" he asked.

"Not much more than that. Can it wait?"

"It's personal, not business."

"Oh, then, of course." Janet sat down at the conference table. She had wanted to take an hour before meeting Mary to start looking at spring suits, but if a friend wanted to talk to her about something, she always put everything else aside. And as a result, everyone in the office brought their personal problems to her. "What is it?"

"Alan tells me that I'm about to be named co-respondent in a divorce suit."

A divorce suit? Michael? Who on earth—

Oh. It was *her* divorce suit.

"Michael, I..." Janet felt uncomfortable. Michael seemed utterly unembarrassed, but she felt uncomfortable.

"Alan made it sound like Wiley was swinging from the chandelier, a breath away from stoning you. I assume it was a little more low-key than that."

"Of course it was," she said hurriedly. "All he said was that you and I seemed like good friends."

"Which we are."

"He didn't mention an affair, and I know he doesn't believe it; I am sure of that. It's just that some friends of ours are having some problems, and we...well, we're not having problems like that, but—"

"POW wives always say it's a bit of an adjustment having their husbands home again."

Not a bad parallel. The U.S. Oil case had sometimes seemed like a war, and Wiley certainly had been a prisoner to it.

Except that it was a prison he had chosen. "I'm sure that things will sort themselves out soon enough," she told Michael. "Certainly my devotion to you is not the issue."

Michael stood up. "It didn't quite ring true to me that he would suspect you of something like that."

"Nor to Alan," Janet said lightly. "He couldn't believe that you were named, not him."

"He mentioned something like that."

If Janet knew Alan at all, he hadn't just mentioned it, he had gone on for hours and hours, treating it all like a big joke. That was like him.

Except it wasn't a big joke. It wasn't at all. It was actually pretty horrible.

Oh, she didn't believe that Wiley had been seriously accusing her of adultery. She could just imagine how she would react, how hurt, how stricken she would be if he had distrusted her in that way.

But that didn't mean this wasn't serious. With everything that had happened to Mary and Tim, Sarah and Dan, Wiley was worried. For the first time it had occurred to him that maybe their marriage was in trouble as well. The thought probably confused, maybe even frightened, him.

But Wiley was not one to admit to confusion and fear, and so when he had spoken, trying to tell her of his awakening concern, it had come out all wrong, as an accusation rather than a plea.

Janet understood that, and she didn't resent it. Wiley was not perfect—although he tried desperately hard to be so—and it was his failings, his limits, that Janet loved as much as his achievements. Just as he had been inarticulate in his grief for his mother, so too was this accomplished, polished man unable to tell her that he was frightened at the thought of losing her.

He had done much to make her angry this last year, but this she understood and accepted.

And suddenly Janet felt guilty. She should not have told Alan about this. She hadn't explained what had truly happened. She had spoken of accusations, making Wiley seem like a jealous, overbearing fool.

Her husband was confused, troubled, and she had made him sound contemptible. Surely that was nearly as disloyal as having an affair.

Mary was waiting. She had already ordered a healthy size carafe of wine. "I hope you don't mind the house wine. I'm so numb these days that everything tastes the same."

"All wine tastes the same to me." Janet poured herself some.

"But you two serve wonderful wine."

Janet laughed. "No, we don't. Wiley serves wonderful wine. I just wash the glasses."

"That doesn't exactly sound like the perfect upscale young professional couple. You're supposed to be training for a marathon together or at least spending Sunday morning in the kitchen together, chopping scallions for a marvelous little omelet."

"You read too many magazines," Janet told her. "Wiley and I never do anything together, we never have."

"Not even sex?"

"Are you kidding? Mary, this is Washington.

Nobody in Washington has sex...except the congressmen."

"And me."

It had taken Janet awhile to get used to Mary joking about her affair. "*Married* sex; nobody in Washington has married sex."

"That's true. Not even the congressmen do that."

But Janet had not come to exchange light banter with Mary. She got enough of that in the office. "So tell me," she said, "how are you? How's living alone?"

Mary twisted a strand of the long blond hair that she wore down and swept over one shoulder. "Are you kidding? It's exactly the same as living with Tim. I get up in the morning, get dressed, have a cup of coffee and some low-fat blueberry yogurt; at night I come home, get undressed, and have a Lean Cuisine and a Tab. How's that any different than what I did all last year?"

"Are you seeing more of George?"

"Actually, I'm seeing less of him. I'm not really sure that I like him very much."

Janet wasn't surprised. She had never met George Landis, but nothing Mary had ever said about him had made it sound like he was irresistible. He had simply been there. "It never seemed like you were all that emotionally involved with him."

"I'm not...although I did just tell Tim I was thinking of living with him."

This was a surprise. "Are you?"

"Oh, no. Didn't I just say that I wasn't sure that I liked him?"

"I may be a little dense here," Janet said, "but if you don't like the man, why did you tell Tim you were thinking of living with him?"

"I'm still trying to figure that one out," Mary admitted. "I guess it was that when I went over to our apartment Sunday night to get my spring clothes, Tim asked me to stay for a drink, and I nearly stayed for the night."

"And that was a reason for telling him that you were going to live with George?"

"It seemed so at the time."

"That must have been an interesting reasoning process. Anyway, Mary, it's February," Janet pointed out. "You don't need your spring clothes yet."

"You know how unpredictable Washington weather is." But Mary's smile acknowledged how trumped-up her excuse was to visit her husband. "You know, I hadn't even decided whether or not to tell Tim about George, but he came home from Houston with this big 'I've been working so hard, be nice to me' attitude that I just had to say 'Wake up, baby, you've made some mistakes.'"

"It did wake him up. In fact, it woke Wiley up too. Did you know that he asked me if I was having an affair with my boss?"

"Wiley?" Mary set her glass down so sharply that the wine sloshed over the rim. "Wiley asked you that? I don't believe it. What's wrong with him? Doesn't he know that you are from Missouri?"

"He's always done his best to forget it." Janet didn't feel disloyal telling Mary this. Mary would understand. "He really doesn't believe it; finding out that you had left Tim made him realize that while he might be in the middle of an entirely perfect career, maybe his marriage isn't so great. I think he didn't know how to say that he was worried."

"Tim didn't either," Mary agreed. "So we are forgiving him?"

"Not entirely," Janet admitted. "I can probably forgive him for asking if I was having an affair, because I'm sure he doesn't believe it—and you really can't expect men to be as open about their feelings as women are—"

"Why can't you expect that?" Mary interrupted.

"Because you'll be disappointed, that's why."

"Good point. So what were you saying about forgiving Wiley?"

"That what I can't forgive him for is asking about Michael."

"What do you mean? Because you work with him?"

"No, not that. I don't see anyone except the people I work with; it would have to be one of them. No, his thinking that it would be Michael just shows he has no idea at all of what goes on in that office, that he has never paid one scrap of attention to the people that I have been working with for years and years. If I were going to have an affair with someone there, it would be Alan, our creative director, not Michael."

"Alan Rule? The tall dark one? Kind of skinny?"

"That's him. The thing about Michael is that he is a whole lot like Wiley and Tim and Dan and—"

"For all our complaints, they are faithful husbands...at least sexually faithful." Mary sighed. "But it's only because they're too tired to play around."

"That's certainly true," Janet agreed. On the rare occasions Wiley had been home during the U.S. Oil case, he had often been too tired to sleep with her, much less anyone else. "And they all have such high-flung notions of their own characters. Cheating on your wife is something only other people do."

"And Alan is not like that?"

"Not a bit. He's perfectly capable of getting very drunk, declaring undying love for me—or any other woman—and then having a wonderful time feeling guilty the next morning."

"And what would you do if Alan got this drunk?"

Janet smiled. "I suppose it would very much depend on just how drunk I was."

"Oh, come on," Mary scoffed. "You'd never do anything like that. It's only tarts like me who would."

"Mary! Don't talk that way about yourself."

When she was working or reading, Mary wore glasses with large peach-colored frames which dipped below her cheekbones, but now, without them on, she looked very vulnerable, and, even when smiling, very sad. Janet reached over and covered her hand.

"Oh, God, Janet, what a mess things are in." Mary tilted her head back as if she were trying to keep tears from falling down her cheeks. "And here I thought Tim and I were perfectly suited because we're both screwed up in the same ways."

Mary was very cryptic about her past, but unexplained comments about a stepfather, about a year spent with an aunt, had told Janet that Mary's life hadn't been easy. "What do you mean?" she asked.

"Oh, the usual. You've read all about workaholics, haven't you?"

"That," Janet said, "is a word we are not allowed to use in my home."

"Workaholic? Why ever not?"

"Wiley says"—and Janet started to mimic him—"that the phrase refers to a pathological condition and most people use it in a careless, uninformed manner to apply to anyone who is the least ambitious and conscientious."

"In other words," Mary translated, "he's denying that he is one."

"You got it. He bristles up when I accuse him of it."

Mary rolled her eyes. "He's a classic case. We all are. Except you, of course."

"Me? I work all the time. How am I any different?"

"Because you work for different reasons. I don't know what they are, just that what explains me and Tim and Wiley doesn't explain you."

"Go on."

"Well, this is probably a lot of psychobabble, but everything on workaholics says it comes, in part, from a fear of intimacy, that people use work to avoid developing relationships with other people. Which is why I figured Tim and I would do just fine. We could spend the rest of our lives at arm's length. I would have thought you and Wiley would split before we did, since he's an arm's-length person and you're a hand-in-hand."

Janet supposed Mary was right; God knows it was hard to get Wiley to talk about things. Maybe that was why she was so close to her friends and her sisters.

"Why do you—" Janet stopped and hurriedly rephrased her question, making it less personal, easier for Mary to answer. "What do the books say about the cause of this? Why are people afraid of being close to people?"

"Loss of control. Intimacy is so bewildering, so unpredictable. That's the thing about the sort of work Tim, Wiley, and I do—it asserts control. If not over people, then at least over a set of facts or a situation. We all need to be able to control what's happening."

Yes, Janet acknowledged, her work was different from that. Sure, the administrative part of her job involved control, but that was just a necessary nuisance. The good part, creating the ads, was, to use Mary's words, bewildering and unpredictable.

"The rest," Mary went on, "is not knowing how to be intimate."

"What do you mean 'knowing how to be intimate'? What's to know?"

"Oh, heavens, the world. I mean, there's—" Mary broke off. "You've always had scads of female friends, haven't you?"

"Yes. I still do." Besides Mary, there was Jody who worked at another ad agency, Ellen and Terry from the house she and Wiley had lived in, and

Bobbi from the congressional office. She could talk to any of these women.

"Although I don't know," Janet suddenly corrected herself. "It seems like I hardly ever see any of them anymore." The only people she talked to these days were Alan and Michael.

"Well, I've never had many women friends," Mary said. "Not until you, and you've got to admit that all this friendship was your doing, not mine. You knew how to get close to a person; I didn't."

Janet shrugged and reached for the wine, and as she did, happened to glance at the mirrored wall behind Mary. It reflected the back of Mary's blond head, the white tablecloth, the lavender chrysanthemums, and another woman, dark-haired and small, dressed in a suit of winter white and a salmon-pink blouse with loosely tied bow that drifted over a few gold chains.

Is that me? That's not how I look.

Janet was sure that neither her sisters nor her mother had a white wool suit. You can't raise a family in a white wool suit.

But you don't have a family. You have your job. And Wiley. That's it.

Janet blinked and spoke quickly. "Well, if I don't fit the classic workaholic patterns, why do I work as hard as everyone else?"

"You tell me."

Janet shrugged. "I don't know. I guess it's that I feel like the agency needs me."

She did know that much about herself—that she needed to be needed.

Her whole family was like that, always willing to

help out, always volunteering, in Scouts, church groups, every kind of civic association and activity, not just because they were good people, but because they enjoyed feeling needed.

And that was how Janet had felt when she had met Wiley. At first, she had been awed by him; she had admired him from afar rather as one would a movie star... until she realized that he needed her.

Wiley had been adrift that year they were living in the group house; he was grieving for his mother without knowing how to grieve, he was lonely without knowing that he was lonely. He spoke of his father with pride and respect, and they met at restaurants for lunch, for dinner, but Lee never came to visit Wiley at the house, which appalled Janet. Wiley needed a home, he needed someone to be there for him.

So she was, and in return, he loved her.

But after two years of marriage, after Wiley had finished law school, his mourning was over, and it seemed like he no longer needed her.

How Janet had longed for a baby back then. She was ready to be needed in the way a child needs its mother. She loved Wiley, she wanted to share this with him.

But Wiley refused, and the next six months were the worst of Janet's life. She hated their condominium; its white walls and square rooms were blank and impersonal. The people in the building seemed cold—people living in high-rise apartments must protect their privacy, and unfriendliness was often the easiest way. Nor was her work satisfying. Yes, she was helping people, tracking down lost Social Security checks, telling people how to deal with the Veterans Administration, arranging for tours of the White House, but it seemed like work anyone could have done.

So Janet left the congressional office and started at the agency. There she discovered that she had a talent, and the agency needed it ... and her. Michael and Alan needed her in a way that no one ever had before. She wasn't just one more warm body needed to organize rummage sales, to donate blood, to collect tickets at school fairs; for once, she wasn't interchangeable with her mother and her sisters.

Janet had done well at the agency. She had won awards, she had been given an elaborate compensation package, but more important to her than statuettes or stock options was the absolute certainty that she was needed.

"Listen," Mary said as they were finishing eating, "how sorry do we feel for ourselves?"

"Very," Janet answered.

"Then let's have dessert."

It was late when she got home, after eleven, which was very late for Janet. Wiley was still up. He must have been working in the study. He came out into the living room at the sound of the opening door. He still had his white shirt on, but he had changed to a pair of corduroy slacks, more casual than what he would ever wear to work. He didn't come to the foyer, but stopped in the living room, his hands in his pockets.

He was angry. It had taken her years to know when he was angry, but there was no doubt now.

"You got my message, didn't you?" she asked. It was an unnecessary question. A message given to a Hastings & Clark secretary was always passed on.

"You know," he said, "I'm home so little, you might make an effort to be here when I am."

Janet stared at him.

I used to be home so much; all those nights when I'd get home at five fifteen and you wouldn't be home until nine. Why didn't you make an effort to be here then?

"Am I supposed to rearrange my entire life just because you're home more?" she said instead.

"I would have thought you'd want to."

"Why? Why should I want to?"

He blinked, surprised at her question. "So we could spend a little time together."

"And you want that?"

"Of course."

"No, Wiley, there's no 'of course' about it." She took off her coat, hung it up. "If being with me were all that important, you wouldn't have vanished for the last ten months."

"I didn't have any choice. It was work. Not like tonight. That was social. You had a choice."

Wiley chose his battles well. If she had worked late, he would have been just as mad, he would have felt just as abused, just as put upon—Janet was sure of that—but he would have kept quiet about it, waiting for an occasion like this when she couldn't defend herself with the same arguments that he repeatedly defended himself with.

Well, hell. She didn't have to defend herself. "My friends are important to me; it's hard to find time to see them."

"And they are more important to you than I am?"

"At times."

Wiley stared at her, surprised that she would say this. It had always been the unspeakable, the unthinkable. She glared back and started back toward the bedroom.

His voice stopped her. "Our lives might not be this stressful if you didn't work so hard."

"If *I* didn't?"

"Yes." His manner was calm, reasonable. Janet resented that enormously. "You'd have more time for your friends and for—"

"The same could be said about you."

"Well, yes," he acknowledged, "but it is different for you. You don't *have* to work as hard as you do."

"And I suppose you do?" He started to nod and she went on, "Oh, Wiley, that's such complete and total crap. You want to work this hard. We could live on a government salary, lots of people do. You love what you do, so you've convinced yourself that you have to do it, but you won't let me do the same."

"Maybe it isn't appropriate to assess blame—"

How she hated it when he was like this—so careful and patient, as if he were dealing with a stubborn toddler. She would rather that he just blurt out what he was thinking.

"—but the point is that we can't both work this hard and still have any kind of home life."

"Home life!" Janet wanted to hit him. "You've got nerve coming in here and suddenly talking about having a happy little home. Every move I've made to make a home for us, you've resisted."

"But isn't that what you wanted?"

"Wanted is right. Six years ago, I was dying for a house and a baby, a back fence, the whole works. Instead I ended up in a high-rise condominium with a husband I never saw."

"This is just temporary. We can move."

"Maybe I don't want to move anymore." She stared at him. "You know perfectly well why I took this job. There wasn't enough going on in my life. If I'd had a house and a yard to take care of, if I'd had a baby, I wouldn't have switched to advertising. I wouldn't have needed to."

"If you need those things now, there's no reason why you can't have them."

Suddenly she understood. "Oh, I get it. Now it's time for us to start playing Mr. and Mrs. Wiley *D*. Hunt."

He stiffened at the mention of his father's name. "What are you talking about?"

"You're about to be made partner. Isn't that when your father got married?"

"Yes. But I don't see—"

"So now all of a sudden you're ready to be married. You weren't eight years ago, but now you are. So, lo and behold, you're remembering the wife you put into cold storage; you're ready to go down to the meat locker and check her out."

"How can you talk about yourself that way?"

"Because you think of me that way."

"I do not. Is it so odd that now that my career is more secure that I am willing to take on more domestic responsibilities?"

"No, kiddo, you're willing for *me* to take on more responsibilities. It's going to be the same.

When work calls, you'll drop everything and go. Except for the money, it would be like being a single parent.''

''I hardly think—''

Janet didn't care what he hardly thought. "Can you promise me there won't be another case like this Houston one?''

''Of course I can't. But it isn't likely. And one assumes that I'd be a partner. The partners on that case came home on weekends.''

''Coming home on weekends is too little, too late.''

This was endless, pointless. Neither of them was saying anything the other was hearing. No words would every jar Wiley out of his careful calmness, and that perfect-lawyer manner made her so angry, so defensive, that she couldn't possibly explain herself.

Wiley turned away, and Janet glared at the back of his white shirt. All their discussions ended up like this. He thought she was irrational, overemotional, insufficiently analytic. She thought he was an all-around, grade-A son of a bitch.

She said nothing. Nor did he. In a minute, he started to rub the back of his neck.

That wasn't like him. He never did that.

Janet loved his hands; she always had. They were slender, elegant, and masculine, his fingers tan as they slipped beneath his white collar. The light caught the gold of his wedding band.

No, no, she was wrong. Wiley did used to rub the back of his neck. That first year she had known him, when he was grieving for his mother, sometimes he had lifted his hand to his neck.

Her heart had gone out to him then, and she had comforted him. She had admired him, loved him, treasured his need of her.

Was all this lost? Was there nothing left but a half-remembered tenderness for how vulnerable even the strongest man sometimes seems?

Janet went into the office very early the next morning; she had a stack of administrative details to take care of. She didn't particularly enjoy that side of her job, but she was good at it, certainly better than anyone else in the Creative Division was.

But she had trouble concentrating. She kept thinking about last night. Quitting her job wouldn't help, she was sure of that. There was just too much else wrong with her marriage besides the fact that she worked hard.

Like her pinball machine. She glanced over at the machine; the female singer had a purple mini-skirt, a tight red shirt, and a gravity-defying bosom.

The machine was a Gottlieb four-player King Rock, a good, solid, old-fashioned mechanical. It had a simple symmetrical playfield without any gimmicks except for an interesting double flipper. It had been one of Janet's favorite games in high school.

Michael and Alan had heard her say that once, and four months before her birthday last fall they had started looking for one. The game was over fifteen years old; it had been popular, and they had had trouble finding one that still worked well. But they had found it down on the Eastern Shore, and so on the morning of her thirtieth birthday, she had walked into her office to find it there, the cabinet swathed with a white satin ribbon.

She had immediately shrieked. It was a perfect gift.

Wiley had been in Houston on her birthday, and so he didn't give her the emerald until the weekend.

The emerald was exquisite, a deep green square-cut pendant suspended from three delicate diamonds. An emerald was just the right stone for her; she wore a lot of greens, rusts, browns, and golds.

But still ...

Wiley had bought it at the jewelry store on the first floor of the firm's K Street office building. There wasn't anything wrong with that; it was an excellent store, but Janet couldn't get rid of the feeling that on Friday afternoon he had gone from the airport to the office, stopping to buy her thirtieth birthday present in just a matter of moments.

Wiley loved her; he was her husband, but it was Alan and Michael, the people she worked with, who started thinking about a present for her in July.

Janet did not know what to do. As the two of them worked harder and harder, their relationship got emptier and emptier; therefore, they worked harder and harder. It was an endless spiral, dropping into nothingness.

Something had to change, but she didn't know what she could do. The first step was going to have to come from Wiley. She didn't trust him enough to take it herself. He'd have to do it.

And he wouldn't. There wasn't a chance. He

might have been worried on Monday night, he might be concerned about their argument last night, but by next week he would have convinced himself that nothing was wrong.

Chapter Six

But Wiley was more concerned by this midnight quarrel than he would have ever admitted to Janet. Of course, he tried not to think about it, but as he passed by Dan Stewart's still-empty office the next morning, he couldn't help what he thought.

Did Janet think their marriage was in trouble? How could she think that? There had never been a divorce in his family, or, for that matter, in hers. That was something that only happened to other people.

It must have just been that she was tired. If she weren't working so hard, she would have reacted more normally. As soon as she was less busy, things would be fine again. He didn't need to worry.

In fact, he couldn't worry; he couldn't allow himself to. Concentration was essential in this job. One of the second-year associates had ruined his career during the U.S. Oil case because he worried about his wife being angry or disappointed at the long hours he was putting in. "But we were supposed to go to her sister's," he'd sigh.

Billing rates at Hastings & Clark were too high for the lawyers to have "productivity gaps," as inattention was politely called.

Wiley pulled out the files on the toxic waste case he had been assigned on Monday. Just as he had told Tim, it was a nuisance suit. A farmer, Herb Johnson, claimed that FalCon was dumping waste from its Iowa explosives plant onto his farm. Certainly that was a legitimate complaint if true, because the chemical in question, CS4, did damage land, blocking the passage of nutrients from the soil into a plant's roots system.

Wiley knew that toxic wastes like CS4 were an increasing problem to American industry. What did you do with things that no one wanted? Leaving them by the side of the Oregon Trail was no longer an option.

But in this case, FalCon had a safe, legal, and, as these things go, not too expensive way of dealing with CS4. A geological fault that ran along the Missouri River made the region around the plant too unstable, too susceptible to earthquakes or tremors, for safe burial of toxic wastes, so FalCon sent the CS4 to an abandoned salt mine in Kansas, shipping the highly soluble blue powder in specially designed plastic drums that would not rust out as would steel barrels. As long as there was room in the salt domes, FalCon could store its waste there. When the mines were full ... well, that wasn't Hastings & Clark problem.

And Herb Johnson did not seem to be a problem either. Yes, he did have one soil sample that indicated some CS4 was in his land, but soil assays from more reputable laboratories found no trace

of it, and Johnson's problems were with his livestock, not with his crop, as would happen if there
were CS4 in his land.

But Johnson persisted in saying that he had
seen trucks from the plant driving by his farm at
night, and he was threatening to file a complaint
with EPA, forcing the federal government to start
an investigation.

That did not bother Wiley. He was not afraid of
EPA; quite the contrary. In general, litigating
against the feds was a piece of cake. Justice had
some fine lawyers, but the individual agencies'
staff attorneys were clearly lesser. Wiley often
knew an agency's regulations better than its own
attorneys did.

Just as Wiley was starting to draft a letter to
Johnson's attorney, his secretary buzzed with the
news that his father was on the line.

Wiley picked up the phone instantly. "Dad!"

"Hello, Wiley. Is there any chance that you're
free for lunch today?"

"I can be, sure. Are you in town?"

"Not yet, but I'm at the airport, waiting for the
shuttle. I've got an afternoon meeting at the
SEC."

Wiley got to the restaurant early. He didn't
want his father to have to wait for him, but he had
only been seated for a few minutes when he saw
his father cross the restaurant.

The two Wiley Hunts did not really look alike;
there was no feature-by-feature similarity between them. Lee's thick hair was now silver and
his presence was distinguished, while his son's
manner would still be described as energetic. But

the resemblance was striking. Their builds were similar, they were the same height, and they carried themselves with the same easy grace. Their manners were alike, and they shared a set of gestures. The younger Wiley had often been told how much he reminded people of his father.

And as he watched his father thread his way around the tables, he knew that he was looking at his future.

As futures went, this one looked just fine. There was nothing about his father's life that Wiley did not aspire to.

Except being a widower.

Wiley pushed aside the thought and stood up to greet his father.

They shook hands. "I sat next to someone on the plane," Lee said, "who said that he had heard good things about my work at U.S. Oil."

"*Your* work?"

"Yes. Was I getting a taste of my own medicine?"

"I trust it wasn't too painful."

"Not in the least. I don't mind hearing that people think well of you. I rather like it."

Wiley opened the menu. He liked his father's style—the understatement, the calm, uneffusive way he had of saying "You are my son and I am proud of you." The Barnums danced all over Janet every time she drew a breath—that family was so aptly named, they truly were a circus. Wiley preferred his father's style.

"In fact," Lee went on, "on Monday I was introduced as Janet Hunt's father-in-law."

"What?" That was a surprise.

"Yes, we had to talk to an advertising agency that might have been involved in setting up a slush fund. But that's not the first time people have mentioned her to me; she is apparently very well-respected." Then Lee put on his reading glasses and opened the menu. "Which reminds me. I got the storage bill for your mother's mink."

"Would you like me to pay it?"

His father looked up over his glasses. "I think I can pay it for one more year. It may take some retrenching, but I can manage."

Lee Hunt's partnership share gave him an income perhaps twice the salary of the President of the United States. "If you'd like a nice check on Father's Day," his son offered, "just let me know."

"I certainly shall. But I wanted to remind you that the mink was there just in case Janet wanted it."

Wiley shook his head. "Janet's not the mink-coat type."

"I didn't think she was, but I thought I'd check."

"I appreciate that."

"And I hope you haven't forgotten about your mother's jewelry. There are some very good pieces. It's yours and therefore Janet's. Wouldn't she like some of it?"

"I don't know. I've never asked her."

His father did not react. Wiley didn't expect him to, since Lee Hunt never reacted to anything—that was part of the blue-chip, law-firm style—but Wiley could hear how surprising his own answer had been. For eight years all that lovely jewelry had been hidden in velvet cases in a dark safe-deposit box, and yet he had never asked his wife if she would like any of it.

"I understand why you gave none of it to her at your wedding," Lee went on, providing an answer to the "Why not?" question that he would never dream of asking. "Your mother hadn't been dead a year, and I know you were respecting my feelings—"

Both father and son knew perfectly well that that wasn't true, but they liked messy emotions to have tidy explanations.

"—but I wanted to assure you that that's hardly an issue anymore. Of course, you may want to save them for your children."

Now Lee was giving Wiley an easy explanation for why he might not want to give the jewelry to Janet at all. It was an extraordinary way to have a conversation, but Wiley was very used to it.

He opened the menu. "We really haven't talked about it."

They ordered, and then as Lee returned his glasses to his breast pocket, he asked, "Speaking of children, are the Barnums putting much pressure on the two of you to start a family?"

"Actually, they don't," Wiley answered. He had never thought about it, but Janet's parents never spoke to them about having children even though Janet was the only one of the Barnum children who did not have children of her own. "It's rather surprising when you think about it because they are so family-oriented and all. I guess it's that they already have a whole herd of grandchildren."

"And it would, of course, be beneath me to point out that I do not."

Wiley stared at him in surprise. What was his father saying? That he thought it time for Janet and him to have a child?

This whole conversation had been unusual. His father always asked about Janet—"I hope that Janet is well." Wiley always said that she was, even if she wasn't, and that had been the end of it. This business of giving her the mink and the jewelry—it seemed strange.

His father had never criticized Janet, not once. But Wiley suspected he had been gravely disappointed when he learned she was to be his son's wife. She must have seemed like the most thoroughly ordinary sort of Midwesterner with nothing at all wrong with her ... except that she wasn't what any of them had ever had in mind for Wiley.

Was that why Wiley had never given her the jewelry? Had his secret knowledge of his father's opinion unconsciously influenced the way he treated his wife?

But Janet's success—even if it was only in advertising—had clearly made Lee think about her more. She was a Hunt now.

They changed the subject, and it wasn't until they were leaving the restaurant that Wiley heard himself bring the conversation back to more personal matters.

"What's the divorce rate among the associates at your firm, Dad?"

Lee made an unhappy sound. "It's shocking. We worry about it, but I don't know what we can do. We can't lower our standards just because the wives are acting differently.''

"That's what some of the older partners at our firm say. 'Our wives didn't divorce us,' they grumble.''

"Ah, but it was all different then.''

"You mean because of feminism and all?''

"Not particularly. Look at your mother, Wiley. She grew up in the Depression; her father was out of work a lot, and you know that the boy she was first engaged to was killed in the war. She would have endured anything for the kind of stability and security that my job provided us.''

"Did she complain about your working too hard?''

"No. She hated it, of course she did, but she knew that not working at all was worse. Young women today don't know how bad things can be. They grew up with more, and so they expect more. You can't fault them for that.''

"But where does that leave my generation? How are we supposed to stay married?''

"Well, you've certainly found a way.''

By having a wife who works as hard as I do. What kind of answer is that?

But, of course, Wiley didn't say that. He could talk to his father about his "generation"; he couldn't talk to anyone about himself.

Chapter Seven

One of the things Wiley loved about working at a firm like Hastings & Clark was that little, routine cases could suddenly blow up into something important. Like this toxic waste case out in Iowa. He had expected it to be nothing, just a minor time-waster, valuable only because it was his first Fal-Con case, but the other side was being annoyingly persistent. The farmer's attorney was trying to make a reputation for himself, suggesting that FalCon was lying, had fudged the other soil samples, and was generally in business for the sole purpose of ruining farmland. He said this to reporters, and little comments began to turn up in the papers.

This was more than FalCon was going to endure. They worked with too many dangerous chemicals, the kind that gave people cancer when they just said the chemical's name, and the company spent too much money carefully disposing of those chemicals to have its reputation soiled by this case. So the client issued the directive dear to the heart of all corporate attorneys: "Stomp them; hang the cost."

The stomping capacity of a major law firm would stagger most Americans. With nearly limitless resources of time, intelligence, and money, the attorneys could tangle up a case, delaying it for years, or they could mobilize a squadron of lawyers on just hours notice, sending one to each of the fifty states if some obscure workings of the federal system demanded it. They could track down judges on fishing trips; they could get midnight phone calls through to the Attorney General; they could tie up the lines of credit of major industrial firms.

Wiley couldn't imagine himself at any other kind of firm. Where else could you walk down the street in the morning, knowing, just knowing that the other guys didn't stand a chance because your work was so good? The government lawyers would have gone home the night before, spending the evening playing with their children, while through the night, Hastings & Clark lawyers would be working. Young lawyers from the top of their law school classes, who, while editing their school's law reviews, had learned to assimilate phenomenal quantities of material; men with the intellectual stamina matched only by the physical endurance of a Pony Express rider; who, at thirty-one or thirty-two, earned what a United States Senator did, backed up by a computerized law library, by secretaries with crackerjack skills and the most advanced word-processing equipment—by every kind of support imaginable; who could turn out a document overnight that would leave the government gasping.

Only in a large firm could you do this sort of

work, only when the client was facing such high stakes that he couldn't worry about his legal bill, when the amounts of money involved were so staggering that even a million dollar legal bill was insignificant, only then could a lawyer perfect his craft, only in such a practice could he attend to every single detail, catch every needle in each haystack.

And when you did that—it was a thrill like no other. Nothing academic, athletic, even sexual could compete with such moments. Nothing. And no price seemed too high to pay. Such lawyers sacrificed youth and fitness, friendship, community, and church.

As winter became spring, Wiley Hunt was at last starting to admit what his wife already knew, that he, like his colleagues, was sacrificing his marriage. He could no longer go on, shoving the thoughts aside, ignoring them, thinking that this was something that only happened to other people. It was happening to them.

There was little left between them.

"What shall we do today?" One of them would say each Sunday.

"I don't know. Shall we do something together?" It wouldn't matter which one was speaking which part; the script was always the same.

"I'd like that. What would you like to do?"

"I don't care. What would you like to do?"

Even as the weather grew warmer, they could never think of anything to do together. Janet didn't play tennis or golf; Wiley was uninterested in hiking or camping. They didn't even have obligations to share. They didn't have children to take to the zoo; they didn't have yard work that needed to be done. There was no reason for them to paint the study together or wash the car. They paid other people to do such things.

They couldn't even fight about money. Their financial decisions were largely limited to how they should invest what they made, and whenever Wiley brought that up, Janet instantly glazed over and told him to do whatever he thought best.

Work had ruined them for leisure. They were too used to goal-directed activity, to tasks that had to be done, to activity that accomplished something. Renting a boat and paddling down the canal, visiting a museum they'd been to before, taking an aimless drive through the Maryland countryside, all seemed pointless, a waste of time. They couldn't relax and enjoy a moment for itself; even in leisure, they expected to be accomplishing something.

So they would work. They were two acquaintances sharing the same residence. The best that could be said about their marriage was that they didn't get in each other's way.

Except for that one night after Janet had dinner with Mary, there had been no dramatic scenes, no fights, no stormy quarrels. This was one marriage that wasn't burning out in flame-hot hate; no, theirs was simply dying, slowly sinking into cold, gray ash.

And Wiley knew it. He loved Janet, but that no longer seemed enough. He wasn't even sure if she believed that he loved her.

He remembered the Browning poem that he had read to his mother:

God be thanked, the meanest of his creatures—
Boasts two soul-sides, one to face the world
with,
One to show a woman when he loves her!

Was he utterly forsaken? Below the meanest of
God's creatures? That he was no longer able to
show this woman that he loved her, that he no
longer thought of goldenrod and sunlight when
he spoke to her? Had the side of him that faced
the world, that was an associate at Hastings &
Clark, that wore the right suit, had the right manner, the right style, had it utterly consumed all
else about him?

But he didn't know what to do. He felt helpless,
a feeling he hated. He who liked to be in control,
who liked power and authority, he felt helpless.

So he worked.

The FalCon case was starting discovery pro-
ceedings during which each side began to gather
evidence. Hastings & Clark adopted a very simple
tactic. They inundated the opposition with paper.
If the opponents made a request, hoping to see a
letter or so, Hastings & Clark would interpret the
request as broadly as possible and would tell Fal-
Con to send over a couple of file drawers worth of
letters. It meant that the opposition's legal bill
soared as their lawyers had to sort through all
those papers, looking for what was relevant. And
one thing a company like FalCon had was an un-
ending supply of boring files.

The farmer's attorneys retaliated by taking far
too many depositions. They simply wanted to

waste the time of FalCon's top executives, and they insisted on sworn testimony even from those who barely knew that this enormous conglomerate had a little explosives plant in western Iowa.

Although he suspected it was too little, too late, Wiley sent someone else to sit in on the depositions. Indeed, it had been a pointless concession. Janet had to fly out to California to rescue an over-schedule, over-budget shoot, and so she was out of town when he would have been.

But he still read each of those depositions even though questions were random, diffuse, clearly designed to irritate FalCon and Hastings & Clark. But a firm like Hastings & Clark never cut corners. You would know, every instinct would tell you, that it was pointless to read something, that it said nothing, that it was a complete waste of time. But you always read it. Always. Too many cases were settled favorably simply because one side's lawyers were more diligent than the other's.

So Wiley read them, the depositions of secretaries, dock loaders, janitors, vice-presidents, the same questions, the same answers, over and over.

At first it was just a feeling of unease, nothing conscious, nothing certain, but as he read the depositions again and again, he started to notice a pattern in a few. Most were unequivocal: "The CS4 goes to the salt mines. All of it." But then there were a few others: "The CS4 is shipped," or "All the CS4 I've handled."

Subtle distinctions, suddenly careful language in an otherwise careless account. Why were these people speaking as they were?

It was only a hunch, but when the client doesn't

care about a few extra hours of an associate's time, you can follow hunches, and Wiley started looking.

Every piece of paper that had poured out of Fal-Con had been processed at Hastings & Clark. Everything sent to Johnson's lawyers had been put on microfiche and indexed and cross-indexed on a computer. That was the way Hastings & Clark did things. So Wiley started going through documents, letters, memos, billing schedules, invoices, EPA permits, contracts, purchase orders, just looking.

Finally he found something. FalCon transported CS4 in specially constructed plastic drums. Three times an order for the drums had been changed; a purchase order had been written and then a few days later rewritten for a lesser number. It could have been a simple clerical error, but why did it keep happening?

As he peered at the screen of the microfiche reader, he could just barely see, handwritten on the corner of one of the canceled purchase orders, the words "steel b's."

"Steel barrels." Steel barrels rusted. Even in the salt mines, the CS4 was stored in more expensive plastic.

"Steel b's" was hardly evidence, but it turned a hunch into suspicion, and once he knew what he was looking for, he was able to piece it together. And within a few hours, he was certain. The plant was dumping some of that CS4 somewhere else.

Probably not on Herb Johnson's farm. There still wasn't any hard evidence of that. But those strange trucks he had seen going by might well have been carrying CS4 to somewhere else, carrying it in steel barrels. Rust would eat holes into the barrels, the wind would blow the blue powder across the fields, the rain would wash it through the soil, and everything that Johnson and his lawyers were saying would come true. FalCon was dumping CS4, and if they were doing it in Iowa, odds were that they were ruining some farmland.

This was Wiley's case, but it wasn't his client. The partner in charge of the entire account handled matters like this.

So he went straight to Robert Wellsmith with the news.

"They didn't perjure themselves, did they?" Wellsmith looked concerned.

"I doubt it," Wiley said and explained what he thought had happened in the depositions. He really believed that FalCon executives knew nothing about it; this plant was just one of many. Probably only a few people at the plant itself would have known.

"I'll look into it," Wellsmith assured him.

And Wiley knew that he would. In the worst possible case if the client said, "Yeah, we were breaking the law; we knew we were doing it, and we don't care, we're going to go on," Hastings & Clark would have to withdraw from the account, but, Wiley thought confidently, there was little doubt of that happening. FalCon was a good client, a company run by well-meaning, prudent people. He was sure that the FalCon executives knew nothing about all this, and he was equally sure that they would much prefer to learn about it from their own attorneys than from the front page of *The Washington Post.*

A few days later, Wellsmith called him in. Yes, everything was exactly as Wiley had suspected. The plant manager had had his eye on the bottom line; he wanted to keep his costs down, and he thought he could cut a corner here.

FalCon ordered the plant to stop immediately, and everyone who knew about it was being fired. The client was acting just exactly as they should, and there was no reason for Hastings & Clark to stop representing them.

"Where were they taking it?" Wiley asked.

"Nearly in their backyard. Over to the next county."

"But isn't that prime farm country?" Wiley's knowledge of Iowa had grown considerably in the last few days.

"How would I know?"

Wiley knew. It was farmland, and somewhere in the middle of that county was a dump of CS4, waiting for rust to free it from its barrels.

"They're going to clean it up, aren't they?"

"Of course. They'll get what barrels are still there."

"What do you mean?"

Wellsmith shook his head. "In the last year or so they've been reusing the barrels."

"They've just dumped the powder?"

Wellsmith nodded, but as Wiley started to speak again, the partner stiffened. "They aren't breaking the law anymore. That's all that concerns us."

"But—"

"I think that's all we need to say about it. It's not our place to make judgments."

"They aren't cleaning it up, are they?"

Wellsmith looked at him for a long moment. "Wiley, they don't know how."

Wiley walked to his office slowly. There were plenty of times when a Hastings & Clark lawyer said to a client, "You'd better not do that anymore." If the client agreed, as they usually did, that was the end of the matter.

And that was happening now. What was different this time?

That it was farmland? Did that make a difference?

Like many city children, Wiley had grown up rather oblivious of farms. Fruits and vegetables came from the produce counter of the supermarket; the relationship between a milk carton and a cow was a theoretical issue.

But his in-laws, the Barnums, felt differently. Both Peg and Dick Barnum had been raised on farms, and they had taken their children to visit the grandparents every month. The whole family revered farmland; they believed it the nation's most precious resource; erosion, bad land management, anything that wasted the land, they felt as keenly as other people felt the destruction of fine old buildings.

And, to Wiley's surprise, the years of living with the Barnums' daughter made a difference to him.

FalCon might not know how to restore the contaminated soil, but they employed some of the nation's best industrial chemists. If anyone could figure out how to do it, FalCon could. And the federal government could force them to do it or to make restitution to the local farmers.

But before the feds could force FalCon to do anything, before EPA could step in, they had to know about it. And they didn't.

EPA had every scrap of evidence that he had, Wiley told himself. Johnson's lawyers were giving them everything. They ought to be able to figure it out.

But no, they wouldn't, he was sure of that. The government lawyers were underpaid, understaffed. They didn't have the luxury of following hunches as he had; they didn't have all those documents computer-indexed; and they probably only had paralegals paging through them anyway. There wasn't a chance they'd find out.

And Wiley could not tell them. That was absolutely clear. The American Bar Association had a code of ethics; a lawyer reported his client's criminality only when someone else's life was in danger, and report after report said that CS4 in the soil wasn't going to hurt people.

Wiley believed this code to be entirely proper. People cut corners; people broke laws. A person had to be able to say to his lawyer "I did this, this, and this, but I didn't do what they said I did." If a lawyer had to report every crime a client had committed, people would have to lie to their lawyers, and it would be nearly impossible to ever mount a defense.

This confidentiality wasn't just a convenience for the large corporations Hastings & Clark represented; it was even more important at the other end of the fee scale. A street kid, railroaded by an overworked cop, needed to be able to be straight with his court-appointed lawyer; he needed that privilege even more than FalCon did.

And what was balanced against this canon of ethical conduct, this foundation from which the legal profession derived the trust and respect of the public, was some Iowa farmland. Perhaps just an acre or two, but conceivably an entire county might be lost.

Wiley had never been to Iowa; he didn't know why he ever would. What was Iowa to him?

And again he thought of Janet's family. Those Vietnamese refugees they had taken in, what had they been to them? The Scout troop in Appalachia they had raised money for, what had it been to them?

What was Iowa to him? Part of his country.

You ask a lot. For on the same side of the scale with the canon of ethics was Wiley's career. If he went to EPA, he would have to leave Hastings & Clark. If he didn't resign, they would fire him. They would have to; the client would insist on it, and Hastings & Clark could not be known as a firm that could not control its associates.

He could never work at a firm like it again. Not after having done this. And he had no idea what he would do. Law was all he knew; this kind of law was all he cared about.

What was Iowa to him?

He pulled out a folder, hoping to work on something else, but he couldn't. He reached for the phone. In a moment—"This is Wiley Hunt. Is my wife there?"

Be there, oh, Janet, please be there.

She was. "Wiley? What's up? Do you have to go out of town?"

How sad that seemed, that she assumed he would call her during the day only if he was going to be traveling.

"No. I wondered if you could meet me for lunch today."

"Lunch?" Janet sounded stunned. "Lunch? You want to have lunch with me?"

"I'd like to."

"Just tell me where."

Chapter Eight

Why on earth did Wiley want to have lunch? In the entire time they'd been married, he had never called her for lunch. Not once.

But she wasn't at all sure it was a good sign. People who were getting divorced had lunch together.

Her face must have betrayed her because when Wiley sat down across from her, his eyes looking serious and tired, he smiled quietly. "You can relax. I'm not here to discuss a divorce."

"Good."

"At least I think I'm not."

She liked it better the first time. "What is it, Wiley?"

But the waiter came, asking if they wanted drinks. Neither did, and Wiley motioned him away.

"Have you ever thought what it would be like if I didn't make partner?"

"Wiley!" Had she heard him right? "No, I mean, not seriously."

He raised his eyebrows inquiringly.

"Well, sometimes," she explained. "I mean,

I've wondered how you'd handle it. I can't imagine you falling apart, but on the other hand, that firm is your whole life. I don't know what you'd have if you didn't have that."

And his expression was so odd, so bitter, that she insisted he tell her what was going on. "Has something happened? You were so sure that you were in. Why wouldn't they make you partner?"

"It's worse than that. I may have to leave the firm."

"Leave the—Wiley, why? What in the world has happened?"

And he told her, about a big company, which he carefully did not name, how one of their minor subsidiaries had been dumping toxic wastes, how the company would stop, but they wouldn't clean it up, not unless they were forced to.

"Why not? Is it like Love Canal or Times Beach? Are people getting sick?"

"No, if that were the case, then I wouldn't have a problem. But this doesn't hurt people; it just ruins the land."

"The land? What land? Where?"

"Iowa. Madison County, Iowa?"

"But that's farm country!"

The same sad smile crept across his face. "I knew you'd say that."

"What can you do?"

"I can go to EPA, but it would be unethical."

"But—"

"Janet, a lawyer is sworn to act in his client's best interests. He must." Wiley picked up his spoon and, for a moment, used its handle to trace circles in the white tablecloth. Then he looked back at her. "Say we were getting a divorce. Wouldn't you want your lawyer to be looking out after you, wouldn't you want to know that he—or she—wasn't giving you a raw deal because I'm another lawyer? Wouldn't you want to be absolutely sure of that?"

"Yes. Yes, I would." That's what the agency was trying to do with the Rose-Maitland account, to let people know that they could trust their lawyers. People didn't trust lawyers, but the legal system was so complex that a person had no choice but to hire them. You could only pray that you got someone worth your trust.

That Wiley's client was a multinational conglomerate did not change the principle at all.

"It would be wrong for me to go to EPA," Wiley said flatly. "It would be against everything that, as a lawyer, I should stand for."

But this was farmland. Janet had been to Iowa often. Its broad plains had some of the finest soil in the world, rich and black. No state raised more livestock, only a few had better crops.

Every harvest her family had gone down to her grandparents' farm to help with the sweet corn. The cousins sat on the flat bed of the hay rack, shucking the corn in the sun's hot glare while the aunts were in the kitchen, putting up the corn in white freezer boxes, their aprons rippling in the breeze from the whirling electric fan. Sometimes Janet would go with Grandpa and the uncles into the big field, and the green corn plants would be taller than she was, with their coarse, broad leaves brushing against her face.

"How can you tell when the ears are ready to pick?" she would ask.

"Oh, you just know," Grandpa would answer.

And after a while, she did just know.

In high school, Janet studied Latin and she had translated passages about Rome conquering Carthage. The Romans had burned the Carthaginian library and sowed the land with salt, destroying both civilization and nature. Salt pulled the moisture out of plants, making it impossible for anything to grow.

Apparently this chemical company was doing something like that.

So much farmland was being lost; thousands and thousands of acres each year were being turned into highways, subdivisions, and shopping malls. Could any one stand by and see more lost, needlessly, carelessly wasted because a chemical company refused to clean up after itself?

These were hard choices for a man to have to make, and she wished that Wiley hadn't been the one chosen to make them.

"I understand that as a lawyer you can't do this." And she could. Every scrap of information that he had had been gained because FalCon trusted him, had been gained while FalCon was paying him. "But what about you as an ordinary American citizen?"

How odd that sounded. Surely Wiley never thought of himself as an ordinary citizen. He was a lawyer. But did that make standards of right and wrong different for him?

She fingered her emerald pendant, running the

stone back and forth along the chain. "It's wrong to go to EPA," she said at last. "But is it more wrong *not* to go?"

"If I were sure of the answer to that, I wouldn't have called you."

The world blurred, and for a moment, Janet forgot about lawyers and citizens, ethics, farmland, everything. Wiley needed her. That's why he had called. This was the closest he'd ever come to admitting it.

"And," he continued, "if I go through with this, it is going to have an incalculable effect on my life, and therefore, I am afraid, on yours."

Why couldn't he have just said "on *our* life"? Had things become so bad between them that they couldn't even share a pronoun?

Yes, yes, things had become that bad.

"Will you be disbarred?"

He winced. "No. I mean, I could be, but it wouldn't happen. They only disbar people who embezzle from clients, not for something like this. But I'll have to quit the firm, and I'll never be able to get another job like this again."

"Oh, Wiley." Janet ached for him. He had never wanted anything else; his whole life had been geared for this; his whole sense of himself was tied to his job. He had always been a lawyer first; before he was a citizen, a husband, a friend, he had been a lawyer, an associate at Hastings & Clark, and he wouldn't be that anymore.

"And I simply don't know what my prospects are, and I just can't think about it yet . . . I don't know what to think—"

This was Wiley, admitting that he could not think about something. He who prided himself on his intellectual discipline, he who needed to be in control, he was in a fog.

"And," he continued, "this could put a very unfair financial burden on you."

"Oh, Wiley, no, it doesn't. Would you have ever objected if I quit my job and you had to support us?" She was going to say "us" even if he wasn't.

"No, of course not."

"Then what's the dif—" Janet stopped. There was no reason to diffuse the issue with a feminist argument. "We won't have to sell the condominium or anything like that, will we?" She really didn't think she'd mind getting rid of it.

"No. A lot of our expenses are discretionary, things we can easily cut back on."

As they ordered and then ate, they talked about practical matters for a while, and while they planned, they realized that the decision had been made, that Wiley Hunt, traditional, conservative, pin-striped to his soul, whose heart was probably dark burgundy with a discreet navy club pattern, was going to rat on his client.

It was against everything he had ever thought he believed in. The ethical conduct appropriate for an attorney had always provided adequate moral guidance for him just as it had for his father. But, for the first time, being a good lawyer was not enough, it wasn't right. And to be right, he had to act as no lawyer ever should.

Janet could hardly believe it. "Will it happen

tomorrow?'' she asked. "I mean, will you stay home the next day?'' She couldn't imagine it. What would he do if he didn't go to work?

"If the partners are angry enough, it could happen that way, but I'll offer to stay on as long as it takes to go through my files and reassign my cases and such.''

"What will you do then?''

He looked at her, his eyes dark, sad. "I don't know, Janet. I just don't know.''

Janet ached for him, her husband. Wiley had always known exactly what he was going to do. His whole life had been planned, programmed, like a six-lane toll road surging across the landscape, all the little hills leveled, all the curves straightened so that nothing could interfere with the blasting speed at which he traveled.

But the expressway had suddenly vanished beneath him, and now he couldn't even find a path, narrow and twisting, whose course he could follow.

Janet stretched out her hand, and slowly, reluctantly, he took it in his.

"This hasn't been a good year for us, Janet.''

They had never said this before, not to each other; they had never spoken the words aloud. But it was true, Janet knew that. Inertia was keeping them together, a memory of love, a commitment to the form of marriage, although they had let the substance drift away.

"I know of no one who is more loyal than you," he went on, his voice almost expressionless.

"A Girl Scout is loyal; a Girl Scout is thrifty; a Girl Scout is—"

He shook his head, stopping this self-mockery. "I don't want you staying with me out of loyalty... or pity."

"Wiley, I—"

Again he stopped her. "No. Just remember if being married to me starts feeling like your duty, that that's not what I want."

"But there are bad times in any marriage."

"Yes," Wiley acknowledged, "but we haven't had much of anything else."

"Wiley, I love you."

"I know that," he said. And neither of them said it—that loving wasn't always enough.

As they left the restaurant Janet realized there was something she ought to say. "You ought to call your father and talk to him."

Wiley straightened his already straight tie. "I don't see what that would accomplish."

"Wiley! He's your father. You have to tell him."

"He'll hate it; he'll try to talk me out of it."

"He deserves the chance to."

And Janet realized that as dreadful as all this was to Wiley, the very worst part of it would be telling his father.

Being a father had never caused Lee Hunt much trouble. Of course, he had had to sign a great many checks, financing the baggage of his son's life: navy blazers, tennis racquets, dental bills, a little Triumph Spitfire when the boy turned sixteen. But although expensive, Wiley had not been a difficult son. He had never been picked up for drunk driving; he had never gotten a girl pregnant; he had never let the air out of his teachers' tires; he had never shown any interest in bombing the campus ROTC building. His birthday had even managed to draw a high enough number in the lottery so that they did not have to worry about him being drafted. In fact, the only times that Lee had ever worried about Wiley had been when he decided to go to Georgetown Law and then when he married Janet Barnum.

And now this.

"I'll be on the next shuttle," Lee had said after a blank pause. "Will you be at home, or at the office?"

"At home," Wiley had answered, too surprised to protest.

"Dad, you didn't have to come," Wiley said as he opened the apartment door to him a few hours later.

"It occurred to me that I'd never had to rush out and rescue you from some scrape. Every father should do it at least once, and I thought that this might be my last chance."

Was there anyone like him? Wiley again admired his father's smoothness, his suavity. "I wouldn't call this a 'scrape,'" he said in what he hoped was the same manner.

"I didn't mean to say that it was. May I come in?"

"Oh, Lord, of course," and Wiley stepped back to let his father pass through the foyer.

"Janet, my dear, you look well." Lee kissed her cheek.

"I'll leave you two alone," she said immediately.

"You don't need to," he told her. "Not unless you are bored by the talk of two lawyers."

"In general, I am," she replied, "but perhaps not now."

It was a phenomenon that Wiley had noticed before. When people were around his father, they started talking like him, their diction slightly more formal, their sentence structure a little more elaborate.

And I'm letting him down.

"May I get you a drink?" Janet was saying, and then sounding like herself again—"But don't ask for a martini; I can't make those."

Lee smiled at her. "Scotch and water would be fine."

Wiley knew what his father would say, and he said it; that what Wiley proposed to do was wrong. "It is a dangerous precedent for a practicing attorney to set."

It was hard sitting here, listening to him, agreeing with him, but unable to do what he wanted.

"I won't be a practicing attorney when I do it" was all Wiley could say.

"Then you've thought about the personal consequences?"

"Janet and I have talked about it, yes."

"That you'll never be partner at a good firm?"

"I know that."

Lee finished his Scotch and then glanced at Janet. "May I have another of these? I'll certainly get it myself."

She shook her head and took his glass.

When she returned, Lee thanked her and then slowly spoke again. "Wiley, your mother sometimes worried that you were following my footsteps a little too blindly. And if that's the case, if you want off this career path, there are other ways to achieve that."

This was the most personal thing his father had ever said to him. He met his eyes. "No, I don't want out. That's the last thing I want."

"Then you're sacrificing a lot for a principle."

"I know."

"I don't object to your putting a principle over personal considerations, not at all. But you know I believe that there is a higher principle, that of a lawyer's ethics. Son, for a lawyer to violate his client's trust, for him to act—" Lee stopped, for once not knowing what words to use.

What words were there? This was the collapse of all that either of them had ever hoped for Wiley, all they had ever understood about him.

"I respect your feel—your opinions," Wiley said, "but I see this as something I don't have much choice about."

"Then there's nothing more I can say." And there was not a trace of feeling in Lee Hunt's voice. Even at times like this, the style was there.

The next day was, Janet was sure, the worst of Wiley's life. He didn't want to talk about it and told her the details reluctantly, tersely.

Robert Wellsmith, whose standing at the firm depended on the FalCon account, had been nearly irrational. James Dennison, Wiley's particular mentor, had instantly asked Wiley if he had discussed the matter with his father, and when Wiley told him that he had, Dennison knew that there was nothing that could change Wiley's mind and, like the excellent laywer he was, started looking for the best way to deal with the inevitable.

Dennison accepted Wiley's resignation and his offer to stay on for a month, clearing up his cases. Dennison asked him to wait a few days before going to EPA so that Hastings & Clark could warn FalCon and try to hold on to the account. Wiley had agreed, but was quick to assure Janet it made no difference. Even if FalCon confessed and embarked on a voluntary cleanup, he still had to resign. Forcing your client to act by threatening to inform on them was the same as actually doing it.

But FalCon thought that Hastings & Clark was bluffing, and two days later Wiley made an early afternoon appointment with a lawyer at EPA. Before the day was over, FalCon had pulled its business from Hastings & Clark.

By the next day everyone at the firm knew, and whenever Wiley stepped into the coffee room, there was a sudden silence. The partners all thought him a traitor; the associates, a fool. Janet could not imagine how he could endure it.

But enduring it he was, silently, grimly, working hard drawing up memos on each client he had been responsible for, trying to finish up the briefs that were due too soon to be reassigned. He hardly spoke to her, and a few days later Tim Keane called her at her office to say that Wiley was not talking to his friends at the firm either. Tim wondered if he wasn't on the route to a serious depression.

"Wouldn't you be?"

"Yes," Tim answered. "Yes, I would be. But

don't you think he ought to start making plans for what he's going to do next?''

"Yes, I think that, but there's not a blessed thing I can do.''

Janet felt helpless. She felt like all she was doing was spending hours on the phone to her parents and sisters, running up the long-distance bill.

She hadn't told Michael and Alan. She wouldn't mind telling Michael, he would be serious and sensible, just as he always was. But she didn't know how she would stand it if Alan knew. He would treat it as a joke, he would never stop talking about it.

Alan was very competitive, and occasionally he was happy when bad things happened to other people. Well, maybe "happy" was too strong a word, but when he heard about something like that, he would go on talking about it for days, interested in every little detail.

And this—Wiley losing his job—Alan would consider excellent theater indeed.

So Janet didn't say anything. It was the first time in years that she had not shared her problems with the people she worked with.

And then, although she could not have thought it possible, everything suddenly got a great deal worse.

She had come home from work early and as she was sitting in the still-dark living room, the phone rang.

"Is Wiley Hunt there?''

"I'm sorry; he's still at work. May I take a message?''

"Is this Mrs. Hunt?''

"Yes.''

"This is Tom Jules of *The Washington Post*—"

Janet's heart stopped. Why was the *Post* calling Wiley?

"—so your husband's still working at Hastings & Clark?"

"I think you had better discuss that with him," she managed.

Three more reporters had called by the time Wiley got home. He already knew that they were looking for him. A reporter from *The Wall Street Journal* somehow managed to get through the firm's switchboard.

Wiley went straight into the kitchen and took the phone off the hook. "I'm afraid this is going to be in the *Post* tomorrow morning."

"But how—"

"It must have been someone at EPA. No one at the firm or at FalCon wants any publicity."

The phone started its irritating little buzz, complaining about being off the hook. Janet put the receiver in one of the drawers so they couldn't hear it.

They did not sleep that night. Neither even bothered to undress. Wiley went into the study and worked all night, writing a brief. Work was his way of handling all stress, all pressure, and it was a crutch that would, in three weeks time, no longer be his.

Janet cleaned closets.

At last, shortly before five, they heard the thud of the morning paper landing outside their door. Janet saw Wiley take a breath and then walk over to the door, open it, lean over, and pick up the paper.

It was on the front page. The article was short

because only an unnamed source from EPA had anything to say. Everyone else had issued abrupt statements. Wiley had said "no comment," as had the firm. FalCon had confirmed that they had changed lawyers, but refused to elaborate.

"I don't suppose we can hope that this is the end of it," Wiley said.

Janet had been reading the paper over his arm, and now she leaned her cheek against him and started to put her arm around his waist, but he stepped away. "I guess I might as well shower and go—"

The doorbell rang.

Wiley cursed the front desk. At midnight, Janet had thought to call down and tell the receptionist not to let anyone up to their apartment.

The doorbell rang again, a frantic ding-dong, ding-dong as the caller kept his finger on the button.

Wiley strode over and pulled the door open. It was Tim Keane.

Wiley frowned and started to speak.

"Let me in," Tim interrupted. "I know who did it."

"Someone at the firm?" Janet asked.

"Good heavens, no." Tim seemed astonished that she had even needed to ask.

"Oh, of course," she remembered. "The paper did say the source was from EPA."

"And you know who it is?" Wiley asked.

Tim nodded. "It was George Landis, Mary's . . . ah, Mary's—"

"I know who he is."

"Well, he was the one who called the *Post*. I

guess they were all feeling smug over at EPA, crowing that FalCon were such sleezeballs that their own lawyers couldn't stomach them. Landis knew that they were our client, and he really hates us, so he dug a little bit until he came up with your name.''

"How did you find out?"

"Mary called. She was outraged, because she thinks he took what was purely a personal matter and started playing professional games. And I'm sure that that's what happened. I imagine he was very disappointed when it was you, not me." Tim's manner suddenly grew a little awkward. "I'm sorry, Wiley, I'm afraid you're being splattered with a little of the muck I've made out of my personal life."

Wiley shook his head. "The publicity doesn't change anything. And if Landis hadn't done it, someone else would."

"Well, you may be right there."

Tim offered to drive Wiley and Janet to work, pointing out that if he had the sense to skirt the front desk by coming up through the garage, then any decent reporter would too.

And indeed, as Wiley and Janet got ready for work, the doorbell rang several times, and Tim, with all the poise and assurance that his job required, was very pleasant without saying anything at all.

Janet was the first one at the agency. She went into her office, closed the door, and tried to work. On her desk was a cassette that had been delivered after she'd left the night before. It was the music for a florist's radio spot. She had to listen to it. But she already knew what it would sound like—awful. The music needed five violins, and the client hadn't been willing to pay for five violins, so there was one synthesizer. The music would sound like it was playing in a roller rink.

What a relief it would be to work in a big agency without such nickel-and-dime clients. Janet had had enough of renting a palm tree and pretending that the Potomac was the Pacific.

Why was she listening to the music anyway? She was senior writer.

She put down the cassette, went to the coffee room, ate two stale cheese Danishes, and then came back into her office and stared into space for two hours.

Shortly after nine the door opened, and Alan Rule stuck his dark head in. "Isn't The Boyfriend's name 'Wiley L. Hunt'?"

Janet didn't answer. This was just exactly what she had dreaded.

Alan came into the office. He had a *Post* in his hand. "I mean, I just asked because I know that there are two Wiley Hunts making our planet such a pleasant place, and—"

How could he joke about this? "Alan, shut up."

He drew up, surprised. "What's gotten into you?"

She gestured at the newspaper. "You obviously know."

"Janet!"

"Please leave."

She had never spoken to him like this before.

Sure, she had ordered him out of her office before, but with a mocking "Get out of here," said only when she knew he was planning on leaving anyway.

But now she meant it. She couldn't stand to be around him.

"Janet..." His voice was different somehow.

But she didn't care. "Right now." She turned away and waited until the door closed.

In a very few minutes Michael Champion was in her office. He sat down in one of the pale gray chairs, for once not reacting to the clutter spread across the conference table.

"Why didn't you tell us?" he asked quietly.

"I have a right to some privacy, don't I?"

"Of course you do. You just haven't ever seemed very interested in exercising it before."

"Well, I'm exercising it now."

Michael stayed calm. "I think Alan's a little hurt that you kept this a secret."

"*Alan's* a little hurt? Alan?" Janet was amazed. "Is that what matters here? My husband had to make the most difficult choice of his entire life, and Alan's hurt because we didn't consult him?"

"We've all been a part of each other's lives for a long time. It's easier for us to work together when we understand each other's stresses."

Two months ago she would have agreed with him absolutely, but Janet was not going to feel guilty about this. Being able to work together was not the most important thing on the face of the earth. "I think having Alan tease me about this would make the stress a lot worse."

"He means well; he's just uncomfortable when it comes to Wiley. He doesn't mean to make things worse for you."

"Well, he certainly succeeded."

Janet was mad at Alan for being flip, and she was mad at Michael for being calm and detached. She felt like neither of them was giving her much support. She went over to her pinball machine and reached under the cabinet to turn it on. She pushed the red reset button to ring up a game and then pulled out the plunger, releasing the ball. It missed all four rollovers and came rolling down the playfield. She caught it on the tip of the flipper and sent it back up.

"Let's not talk about Alan." Michael's voice was behind her. "Tell me what's going on."

She kept her back to him, playing as she talked, never looking up at the score, never knowing which ball she was on. When the flippers stopped working, she would just ring up another game.

Michael's questions were even, steady. He didn't seem to mind talking to her back.

"Will you be fixed all right for money?" he said when she at last finished her narrative. "The agency can certainly arrange some sort of loan."

She shook her head. "We'll be fine."

"I thought you would be, if Wiley's been handling the family finances."

It had once surprised her that Wiley and Michael weren't friends. They clearly respected each other's judgment, but they had always kept their relationship pleasant but rather distant. Janet couldn't understand that. If you thought you might like a person, why not try to have a friendship with him?

"I'm going to give you a little advice," Michael was saying, "although I don't suppose you want it. This is the name of a reporter at the *Post* who plays straight." Michael laid a piece of paper down on the glass of the machine. "Wiley ought to talk to him, get his side of the story on record."

Janet didn't stop playing. "He won't. He doesn't care." The ball rolled down the center of the play-field; there was no way to keep from losing it. "Nothing anyone says about him could be worse than what he believes about himself."

Michael shook his head. "It's not going to be like that. Listen, I understand the way the media works, I understand what happens to stories like this. Your husband is going to be labeled an environmental hero, and I imagine he'll want to say he's not."

Michael was right. By the next day, the papers had a more complete story; someone at FalCon talked, and Hastings & Clark confirmed that Mr. Hunt had indeed voluntarily resigned. And although no one was willing to go on record as saying "Yes, Wiley Hunt did this," there was no doubt and the papers treated it as a fact.

It was not the sort of story that the papers let die. It raised just too many interesting issues, both environmental questions and problems of legal ethics. So there weren't just news stories, but columns, people thinking about, reflecting on, the matter.

And just as Michael had predicted, Wiley was not regarded as some shyster who had ratted on his client; instead he was emerging as a hero, as a man who stood up for the environment against a hated chemical company, as a man who flaunted the arrogant legal establishment at great personal sacrifice.

He was horrified.

Chapter Nine

Q: Mr. Hunt, when the Kutak Commission proposed changes in the code of professional conduct a few years ago, one change was that a lawyer could reveal information about his client to prevent a crime that would cause substantial economic harm or to rectify the consequences of a client's criminal or fraudulent act. That would have made your actions ethical, would it not?

A: Yes. But that was simply a proposal. The Bar Association House of Delegates deleted those passages before the new code was submitted to the annual meeting.

Q: Do you think that that was wrong?

A: I hardly think I'm qualified to tell the Bar Association what their ethics should be.

Q: Why not?

A: Because the reason for having such a code is so that individuals do not act upon their own discretion and . . .

"You don't have a thing to worry about," Janet told her husband. "You're so boring that no one will read this."

"You're just being nice."

Wiley was lying on his back, staring glumly at a coffee cup balanced on his chest. Janet was propped up on the pillows next to him, reading the Sunday *Washington Post,* most particularly the editorial section, which contained an interview with him. At Janet's urging, he had finally called the reporter that Michael had recommended.

Janet looked over at him. He wasn't moving; he had said little all morning. He had been like this for days.

She suspected that his mind was as blank as he could possibly make it. In his silence, he was desperately trying not to think about everything that had happened.

Janet thought this a mistake. It wasn't healthy for him to keep everything so bottled up. She thought he ought to talk about it. "Wiley, the interviewer did ask you what plans you had for yourself."

Wiley had told the *Post* he had made none, but Janet was hoping he might be more forthcoming with her than with a journalist.

But of course he wasn't.

"I don't want to talk about it."

"Wiley, I think you ought—"

"There's no reason to dwell on it." He put the coffee mug on the nightstand with a sharp little bang and got out of bed, going over to the closet door for his robe.

Janet watched him, hurt and angry that he was so abrupt with her.

It wasn't fair, she thought irritably as he thrust his arms into his robe. He deserved to be fat. He really did. He'd been athletic before he started at the firm, but he got almost no exercise now. He drank hard liquor, he ate quantities of red meat and not nearly enough vegetables. He put cream in his coffee and used real butter. But his body was still lean and muscular.

Janet had to think about her weight every day of her life or she would balloon up beyond all hope. It was not in the least bit fair.

Oh, great, your husband is more miserable than he has been in his entire life, and you're mad at him because he's thin. You're a really swell human being.

The phone rang, and Janet reached to answer it, happy to have something to do. But Wiley stopped her.

"Don't. Let the machine do its stuff. That's why Tim brought it."

A day or so after the publicity had started, Tim had brought his answering machine over to the apartment. They kept the machine on at all times.

Janet listened as the caller left his message. It was a client of hers, the lawyer Roger Rose. She was a little surprised; clients rarely called her at home and never on a Sunday morning.

But obediently she returned the call. "Roger, this is Janet. What can I do for you?"

"Actually, I was hoping to talk to your husband."

"Just a moment." Janet handed the receiver to Wiley.

He frowned at it and she quickly covered the mouthpiece with her hand.

"I don't want to talk to him," he said. "Why didn't you say I wasn't home?"

"At nine thirty on a Sunday morning? Where on earth would you be?"

Wiley raised his eyebrows, silently reminding her that there had been plenty of Sunday mornings when he would have been in the office already.

"He's my client," she whispered. "You can talk to him."

Wiley rolled his eyes, but sat down on the bed and took the receiver. "Hello, Roger, how are you?" The perfect lawyer.

Janet got out of bed to go shower. She had long since learned not to listen to Wiley's phone conversations, hoping to figure out what they were about from what he was saying. Not only did it irritate him, but it was also pointless. It never worked.

When she got back out of the shower, Wiley was standing at the window, his hands in the pockets of his robe, staring out.

"What did Roger want?" she asked his back.

"He offered me a job."

Oh. She knew what Wiley thought of the kind of small-potatoes practice Roger had. "That was nice of him," she said.

Wiley ignored her. "Maybe I should learn Spanish and start an immigration practice."

Janet kept quiet.

There was nothing about Wiley that she disliked more than this. He wasn't without social feeling. He was very conscious that even a capitalistic society had responsibilities for the unfortunate; his politics were the most liberal thing about him.

But he was an elitist. He was perfectly willing to pay taxes and donate to charities so that the poor, the handicapped, the ill-educated, the retarded, could be helped.

But helped by someone else. He felt no identity, no bond, with the disadvantaged. Yes, undocumented aliens needed legal representation, and yes, it was a shame that so few excellent attorneys ever got involved in immigration work, but no, he wasn't going to be the one who did. Attorneys at firms like Hastings & Clark believed that they were doing something superior to that.

But Wiley had now stepped away from that world. What was he going to do?

Roger Rose's call was the first of many that week. Every Ralph Nader-type organization in Washington and New York called him; they would have loved to have him. But Wiley refused. "They do some good, but most of what they do, all their petitions and writs and stays," he said to Janet, "just result in firms like ours making a fortune."

Firms like ours. He was still saying it, still thinking it.

EPA would have been glad to have him, and a former colleague, someone who had not gotten a partnership at Hastings & Clark, called and was surprisingly pleasant, encouraging him to come to the Justice Department. He turned them all down.

"But he's got to do something," Janet said to Mary Keane on the phone. "It's not just the money...although God knows we will miss his income. But he'll go mad without a job; he's only got another two weeks at Hastings & Clark."

"How much weight have you gained?" Mary asked.

Janet dropped the jelly doughnut she'd been eating. Mary had the same food problems she did. When they were under stress, they ate. Janet had tried to put on the skirt to her gray suit this morning. It hadn't fit.

"And why are you telling me this?" Mary went on. "No, you don't have to answer that. I know. You are saying it to me because you can't say it to Wiley."

There had been a time when Janet was almost pleased that all this had happened. When the crisis had come, Wiley had turned to her; he had talked to her during that one long lunch more than he had talked to her in years. Never before had she said that she thought he was defined by his job, never before had he acknowledged that their marriage was in trouble. These were things that needed to be said, and they wouldn't have said them if this case hadn't happened.

But those hours of intimacy had faded. The two of them were more distant than ever. Wiley had completely withdrawn into himself.

He wasn't sleeping. He came to bed very late and got up early. When she mentioned it, he only said that he had a lot to get done. But she knew it was more than that, because when he was in bed, he just lay there, unable to sleep. As large as their king-size bed was, even though it sometimes seemed like he was over in the next county, she knew from his breathing that he was not asleep.

One night she turned over and propped herself

up on her elbow. "Wiley, do you want to talk about it?"

That was stupid; of course he didn't want to talk about it. That was the last thing he would ever want to do.

He didn't even bother to answer.

He was lying on his back, his hands linked behind his head. Desperate for some kind of contact with him, Janet slid across the expanse of bed and put her head on his shoulder. She expected him to lower his arm, put it around her shoulders, hold her to him.

He did not.

"Wiley, will you hold me?"

Slowly the weight of his arm came around her. The skin against her cheek was warm and she ran her hand over his chest. He didn't react. She turned her head and kissed his shoulder, then moved over him to kiss his neck as her hands began to slide down him and—

Strong hands closed around her shoulders, pushing her away.

She was stunned. "Wiley!"

He sat up, pulling the pillow back behind him. "I don't need you to feel sorry for me," he snapped.

"*What*?"

"How long have we been married? Eight years, is it? And just how many times have you taken any kind of sexual initiative?"

"Initiative? But I—"

"Oh, I know," he interrupted. "You enjoy sex, but you never start it. Hasn't it ever occurred to you that I might find it rather gratifying if you did?"

No. Obviously it hadn't. She had never thought about it; she just hadn't. When they went down to the car together, it never occurred to her to drive. She always assumed that he would want to. And just as unthinkingly, just as automatically, she had thought of sex as something he started.

But of course he was right; there was no reason in the world why it should be that way. She was wrong.

Janet felt sick. She hated it when she hurt someone; she really hated it. "But you never said a word."

"What would that have accomplished? Then you would have started out of a sense of obligation, which ranks right up there with pity as one of the great reasons for sex."

"Pity? But I don't—"

"Isn't that the reason for this current burst of affection? That you feel sorry for me? That's great; it's what every man wants, for a woman to go to bed with him out of pity. It's a real thrill."

"Wiley, why are you angry with me?"

"I'm not angry with you. I just find it amusing, that's all."

I just find it amusing, that's all. She hated it when he was like this, so calm and smug and disinterested.

And now that she thought about it, she wasn't entirely to blame. He should have said something, instead of spending eight years feeling abused. How was she to know what he wanted if he didn't tell her?

She thought that he liked it this way, that he liked to be the aggressor, that he had to be in control of everything, including her body.

"Maybe I never start it," she declared, "because I'm not so crazy about what happens."

Wiley froze. "I hardly think you have any grounds for complaint."

"Because you do such a wonderful job, is that it? That's what it feels like sometimes, Wiley, that I have to have a good time so that you can have something else to feel smug about. It's like my having an orgasm is just another one of the goals that you have to achieve to prove how perfect you are."

Wiley flung off the covers. "I think you are not considering the alternatives." He grabbed his robe and jerked open the bedroom door.

"Where are you going?" she demanded.

He didn't answer, but he didn't need to. She knew what he was going to do. He would go down the hall, through the living room, and into the foyer. He would pick up his attaché case and take it back into the study.

He was going to work.

Janet went straight to her pinball machine the next morning. It was either that or rig up an IV for massive transfusions of Fritos and Sara Lee cheesecake.

The machine was so familiar. The pink "Open Gate" light went on when the bonus was at three; the red "Special" lit when it hit eight. It had worked exactly that way when she was in high school back in Missouri, back when she was unhappy because her mother wouldn't let her wear her skirts as short as other people's mothers let them wear theirs. And the machine was still working that way even here in Washington, when her husband's life was falling apart.

The silver ball shot around the red and purple playfield, dancing off the pop bumpers, slipping over the rollovers, zeroing in on the targets. Janet didn't stop even when she heard her door open.

Michael put a quarter on the glass of the machine, the traditional sign for "I want this machine next."

Janet let the ball roll out of play.

"I take it things are getting tense?" he asked.

Yes, yes, they were. And she had to talk to someone. If she hoped to get anything done at all today, she had to talk to someone.

She used to have so many friends, so many women she felt close to, she could have talked to them. But then she had allowed work to take over her life. The only woman she saw anymore was Mary, and Mary could not give her the steady reflection that she needed.

So she had to tell Michael, a man she worked with. There was no one else.

"Wiley and I had a fight last night."

"About what?"

"Oh . . . nothing, really." If Michael were a woman, if she didn't work with him, she could have said what the fight had been about. "He just seemed to want to get angry. He got mad when the paper was late this morning. That isn't like him."

"Denial, anger, bargaining, depression, acceptance."

"What?"

"You've heard that. Elizabeth Kubler-Ross's five stages a dying person goes through."

"Wiley's not dying."

"He probably feels like he is. I certainly would in his shoes. So for a while he was denying that it was happening—you said that yourself. So now he's moving on to the anger stage. And Wiley's too much the Establishment creature to let himself get mad at the Bar Association and he's not the type to sit around whining 'Why me?' So he gets angry with you. It's his only alternative."

"Oh, wonderful."

"Brace yourself. He'll probably keep quiet about the bargaining stage. So depression is next."

"I can hardly wait. When do pestilence and famine come?"

Wiley got angry again that night as he went through the mail. One of his letters was a follow-up to a phone call that he hadn't told Janet about. An acquisitions editor from a New York publishing firm had approached him about writing a book.

"What's wrong with that?"

"They aren't interested in what I have to say," he said bitterly. "They just want to cash in on all this publicity."

"Are you sure?"

"Of course I'm sure," he snapped. "They want a general-interest book on ethics. I don't have a thing to say on that. If they really cared about my opinions, it would be on administrative law, the workings of the regulatory agencies. That's all I know about.''

"Did you say that? Did you suggest that you might write a book about that?''

"Of course not.''

Janet flinched under his crisp tone, but remembered that this anger might be an entirely normal reaction, that it probably had nothing at all to do with what she was saying. She always took everything he said very personally. That was why so many of their discussions got nowhere.

She forced herself to remain calm. "Well, why not? Not a book for lawyers, but for ordinary people like me. There must be things about regulatory law that the average citizen ought to understand.''

Wiley looked at her as if she didn't know what she was talking about.

"You know,'' she went on bravely, "about things like why we don't have red M&M's anymore, what's involved in outlawing red dye number 2, if that's what happened.''

"I am not going to write a book about red M&M's.''

But at the beginning of his last week at Hastings & Clark, Wiley called her at work. "Am I right to assume that you thought this book was a good idea?''

This wasn't exactly the most intimate beginning for a conversation, but it was something. "Yes.'' A book contract would be a bridge, a project for him to undertake while he sorted out his options.

"Well, that editor called again, and I mentioned the regulatory agencies question. He seemed interested and asked me to draw up a proposal."

"Wiley, that's great!"

"No, it isn't great, but it should keep me off the streets."

Chapter Ten

Hastings & Clark did not, of course, give a farewell party for Wiley, but both his particular friends — Tim Keane and Dan Stewart — and his mentor, James Dennison, took him out to lunch during that last week.

Wiley wasn't particularly forthcoming about those lunches, but it didn't take much to make Janet realize what a blessing this book project was. It gave them something to talk about. These men all knew how important regulatory agencies were to the workings of American society, and they suspected that most citizens knew little about them. Wiley's project seemed interesting, important.

They would have managed somehow even if Wiley had had nothing to do on Monday morning — that was part of the Hastings & Clark style — but his starting a project that seemed like an extension of their work made this last week easier on everyone.

Especially on Wiley.

Janet had suggested that the two of them go away that weekend, to West Virginia, perhaps, or the beach—there were lots of weekend spots that they had been meaning to go to for years, but had never gotten around to—but Wiley had refused. "I don't think it would be much fun."

Well, she had to agree with that one; it wouldn't have been fun at all, but she hadn't proposed the weekend because she had wanted to have a good time. No, she had wanted to do something for him, help him through this difficult time.

Janet simply did not know what to do. It wasn't enough to love him; he needed more than that. He needed encouragement, support. But he was resisting every effort she made. She felt helpless.

He started work on the book immediately—Saturday morning, in fact. One of his former professors made arrangements for him to use the Georgetown Law library, and at first he left home every morning just as he had always done, the only difference being that he wore slacks and a blazer instead of a suit. Otherwise, from Janet's point of view, that first week wasn't that much different than when he was working at the firm. He still came home late. He was interviewing a number of government workers; he often met them after work.

He talked to her about the book no more than he had talked about any of his Hastings & Clark cases. This irritated her a little. After all, the proposal had been her idea. But his silence also worried her. He seemed seriously depressed, but how could she help him if he wouldn't talk to her?

Finally at dinner one night, Wiley did speak about it. "I found out about your red M&M's."

"Did you?" Janet tried to sound enthusiastic. "Was it red dye number 2?"

"Actually not. Red M&M's did not have red dye number 2 in them, but a lot of consumers thought that they did so the Mars people stopped manufacturing red candy."

"Just because people thought there was red dye number 2 in them?"

"Sure." And then Wiley smiled; for the first time in weeks, Wiley smiled. "You did it to yourself, Janet. If you and people like you hadn't spread rumors about red M&M's, you'd still have them."

Janet used to hate him saying such things as "people like you"; he sounded so contemptuous and mocking. But right now, she didn't care. She wasn't going to let herself be distracted by taking what he was saying so personally.

"That's interesting," she said instead. "You're going to put it in the book, aren't you?"

He shook his head. "Not at all. It doesn't raise any interesting legal questions."

"Oh."

"Not like the cranberry thing."

"What cranberry thing?" *We're talking; we're actually talking.*

"Just before Thanksgiving—it was back in the mid-sixties, I think—someone got some strange sickness and the tests traced it back to cranberries. One lot of cranberries tested positive for whatever it was they were looking for . . . I can't remember all the details. So the federal government put out a warning that cranberries were contaminated, and not many people bought cranberries that year."

Janet winced. "That hurts. I can't imagine Thanksgiving without cranberries."

"It couldn't possibly have hurt you as much as it hurt the cranberry industry. It put some of the smaller manufacturers out of business. And then it turned out that the tests were wrong, that standard procedures for testing weren't followed, and there wasn't anything wrong with the berries."

"That's awful!"

"The cranberry people certainly thought so. So the question was should they be paid damages for their losses?"

"Of course."

"There's no 'of course' about it because of sovereign immunity," Wiley said. "You can't sue the king ... or rather the government."

"Why not? That doesn't sound fair."

"On some things, people can; the law's changing, but it hasn't on this yet."

Janet frowned. That didn't seem right, but she really didn't know enough about it to make a decent decision. And she was willing to bet that plenty of people were in her shoes. She read *Newsweek* faithfully, but that didn't seem to be enough. The nation was so complex—it was hard to keep up.

"Take heart," Wiley told her. "The Mizokami brothers got paid for their spinach crop."

"Spinach crop? Tell me."

"In 1962, these guys, the Mizokami brothers, sent part of their spinach crop east. FDA agents tested some of it and said two railroad carloads were contaminated with a certain pesticide. The brothers denied that they had ever used it, but they plowed under the rest of their crop—"

"And I suppose a lot of people started calling them the Kamikazi brothers."

Wiley laughed. "Yes, of course. Anyway, the tests were wrong again, but this time the government paid damages. Took an act of Congress to get it, though."

"I think this is something people ought to think about," Janet announced. "I guess that's the point of your book."

He shrugged. "I guess." The drawn, tired look came back to his face as if helping people make informed decisions about the workings of their government were beneath him.

Within another week, he had finished his preliminary research and settled down to write up the proposal, which would consist of sample chapters and an outline.

He was working at home. She felt odd, dressing each morning in one of her increasingly tight dress-for-success outfits, while Wiley put on khakis and Top-Siders. It was even stranger to come home and have him there.

On Wednesday of his first week home, she went into the kitchen and found that he had gone to the grocery store.

"You didn't have to do that," she said. Although she felt that *Ms.* magazine would want Wiley to take over the household chores now that he was home more, she was not going to make an issue of it. This was all hard enough on him anyway.

"I wanted to get out."

"Going a little dingy staying at home?"

"I don't know how housewives do it. Don't they get lonely?"

Janet was impressed. Wiley had never before wondered about how other people spent their days; either you were a hot-shot, killer lawyer or you weren't worth thinking about. "Some of them do get very lonely, but not all." Then hoping that he was eager enough for the sound of a human voice that he might be willing to listen to his own, she asked, "How's the book coming?"

"Okay."

"Just okay?"

"If that."

Janet stared at him; this was as close as she had ever heard him come to expressing any kind of self-doubt. "May I look at it?"

He shrugged. "I don't know why you would want to."

He was fidgeting with the coffee grinder that was screwed onto the edge of the kitchen counter. He whirled the black handle around and around although there were no coffee beans in it. The noise was high-pitched and harsh.

I don't know why you would want to.

This was depression. It was too late for denial; he was done being angry; if he had done any silent, pointless bargaining, she didn't know about it; he was just depressed.

"I'd just like to," she said. "That's all."

"Suit yourself."

So as they sat down to dinner, he handed her the outline and the beginnings of a sample chapter.

"Little is known by the general public of what..."

I. History of regulatory law.

   a. Anglo-Saxon land law...

The sheets of paper were off a yellow legal pad. Across each line were the blue tracings of Wiley's neat handwriting, handwriting as regular and correct as he was. Janet took the paper clip off the outline. She put it back on.

She did not know what to say. This was a textbook, a tome. Perhaps the content was elementary enough for the general public, but the style, the manner, was that of a legal brief. Where were the cranberries, the spinach, the red M&M's?

"I don't know much about book proposals," she began hesitantly, "but—"

He interrupted. "But it's boring."

She sighed, relieved that he already knew. "Oh, Wiley, I'm afraid that it is."

"I know. I can't imagine anyone wanting to read it."

Suddenly Janet felt on familiar ground. One of the first things you had to do in an advertising campaign was establish the target audience. Were you speaking to men? Women? Ages 16 to 21 or 29 to 34? And what was your purpose? Were you trying to get old users to consume more? Were you trying to get new people to try the product?

Wiley hadn't done that; he hadn't thought about his audience. He had no sense of who would read the book... and if he didn't figure that out fast, no one would read the book.

This was why Janet was as good in advertising as she was—there were certain audiences that she seemed to understand. She could communicate to them, she knew what would motivate them to want to find out more about a product, to want to try it, taste it, own it. She could communicate to them because she knew what it was like to be them. She could put herself in their shoes. But Wiley couldn't. He knew nothing about people who would read his book.

Of course not. He only read professional materials; he never read general-interest nonfiction. He didn't know why anyone would want to, what kind of pleasure there was in such books.

She stood up and started pulling on his arm. "Come on, we're going to the library."

"We're what?"

"You heard me. We are going to the library to check out some books."

"The Arlington library's not going to have anything I didn't see at Georgetown."

"No, we aren't going to check out law books; we're each going to get a regular, general-interest book and read it. If we like reading them, we'll figure out why. If we don't like them, then you can't write this book. You can't write what you don't like to read."

She knew what she was saying made sense, and Wiley's eyes seemed to lighten as he listened to her. It was as if he had felt swamped, with failure's sour darkness closing over him, and then she had spoken, promising to show him a way out.

Of course, he didn't say that. "Can I at least finish my dinner?"

"No. But if you read your book, you can have dessert."

The main branch of the county library was just a

few blocks away, and within a few minutes they were standing at the reference desk.

"We'd like to check out a book," Janet told the librarian.

"Two books," Wiley added. "One each."

The librarian looked surprised. "What sort of book?"

"General-interest nonfiction," he told her.

"On what subject?"

"We don't care," Janet said.

The librarian obviously thought this a little odd. "Are you sure you don't have a subject you are interested in?" She looked at them, trying to determine something about their interests from the way they looked. She spoke to Wiley. "There's a good book on Wall Street law firms that—"

"No!"

At the sound, several other people looked over curiously, and Janet tried not to giggle.

Wiley was clearly a little embarrassed. "I mean, I already know a lot about that. I'd rather have a book on something else... Oh, I know, do you have anything on pinball machines or on rock and roll?"

And as the librarian started to bustle over to the card catalogue, relieved to have a manageable request, Janet had to swallow and blink.

Oh, she knew that Wiley loved her, but it always seemed like he was contemptuous of many of her interests. Even her career—he could dismiss it with a flick of the hand because she was in advertising. But now he was making an effort to understand the things she was interested in. He had never done anything like that before.

The pinball books weren't very analytic, mostly

pictures with some history. "There's a market for you, Janet," Wiley said as the librarian sent them upstairs to the fine arts collection where the music books were. "A book about how pinball machines reflect American culture."

"It would be too depressing," she replied immediately. "I hate the machines they make now."

"You do?" Wiley never went near arcades so he wouldn't know.

"Goodness, yes." *He's listening to me; he never listens to me, but now he is.* "For one thing they are dark and confusing, it takes three rolls of quarters before you can figure them out enough to win, and the worst part of it is that the machines talk to you now. Life's tough enough—I mean, I have to work with Alan Rule—I don't need pinball machines to talk back to me."

"The whole country's going to hell, isn't it?" he said sympathetically.

"It sure is."

Wiley got his rock and roll book, and Janet in turn asked for a book on sailing. "Not a 'how-to,' but 'why.' A book that tells how much fun it is to sit in the middle of a boring ocean, when you're cold and wet and have to go to the bathroom."

She riffled through her credit cards to find her library card. It had expired almost a year ago—had it been a year since she'd checked out a book?—and they had to wait in line to get it renewed. But at last they checked out their two books.

After he held open the door, Wiley took the books from her. "I felt like an inner-city kid in a Norman Rockwell painting: 'Please lady, can I check out a book?'"

Not bad, Janet thought. In the space of a single

evening, Wiley had managed to have some empathy both with housewives and inner-city residents. In another week he might turn into Abe Lincoln.

But she wasn't going to make him self-conscious about it. "Don't be silly," she said instead. "Norman Rockwell didn't paint inner-city kids."

It was a soft, warm evening, just now growing dark. A children's soccer game had finished at the park next to the library, the young players exchanging last remarks with their friends as they trailed their parents back to the station wagons. It seemed like everyone had come in cars. These people must live in the residential neighborhoods just a few miles away, on green, tree-lined streets with single-family homes and yards and doghouses.

If only that were us . . .

How nice it would be if they lived in a quiet, pretty neighborhood and took a walk after dinner regularly. Kris, Janet's secretary, and her husband did that every night; that was part of why they had a dog, to force them to get out.

Maybe if we did this, we wouldn't always feel so tired after dinner. But it's such a nuisance in a high rise. If we lived in a house . . . if we had a dog . . .

Back at home, they settled down to read their books, propped up against the pillows of their big bed.

Janet's sailing book had a lot of pictures in it, which was just as well, because Wiley kept interrupting her. "This is interesting. Did you know that—" And he would mention some fact about Elvis Presley or Buddy Holly that she would have thought that the whole world had always known.

She had trouble concentrating on her own book. Wiley was leaning against the low headboard of their platform bed. He was wearing a rugby shirt with stripes of green and tan; the sleeves were pushed up over his forearms, and the placket of the white ribbed collar was open. She moved over next to him.

"Have I seen that shirt before?"

He looked up, surprised. "Maybe not. I think I picked it up in Houston—we were always running out of clothes down there—and then forgot about it."

Janet put her head on his shoulder. He started to read again; he really was interested in the book. She reached over and slipped her hand in the open placket of his shirt, moving her fingertips against him, feeling the warmth of his skin.

"You're making it hard for me to concentrate," he pointed out without taking his eyes off the book.

"I'm sorry," she apologized and showed her regret by pulling his shirt out of his jeans.

"Mrs. Hunt! I'm reading." Wiley closed the book and started trying to beat her off with it.

He failed utterly.

"Janet?"

"What?" she murmured drowsily.

"I love you."

"That's nice." She really was almost asleep.

"No, I'm serious. I do love you, and I don't think I say it enough."

She was instantly awake. They hardly ever talked after making love. It wasn't that Wiley was abrupt. No, he stayed with her and then held her as they fell asleep, but they didn't usually say anything beyond a few endearments.

"Maybe I should go to the library with you more often," she said lightly.

"Among other things."

She understood. It had been different this time. They usually took sex so seriously; making love had been quiet, intense, and dark. But this time, they hadn't gotten around to turning off the lights, and Wiley had made a few wry remarks. And, of course, she had started it.

Janet could so sympathize with his feelings on this. If he never took the initiative, if she always felt like she were asking him to make love to her, she would hate it.

Haltingly she tried to tell him that.

"It is sometimes like that," Wiley admitted. "When you are young, you think of sex as something you have to try and persuade a girl to do. And I suppose it's a rather natural fantasy to want someone to be trying to persuade you, to be the one who is wooed for a change."

"Of course," she managed to say.

Other couples might do this all the time, sit around and explore their sexual fantasies together. He and she certainly never had. The only other time they had talked about sex in any detail had been in anger.

"In law school once," he continued, "some of us were talking about why there were so many lesbian scenes in male-directed pornography. Most people were saying it was just because in the lesbian scenes, there were two—or four—of everything. But I also think that those scenes so clearly show that women have strong sexual appetites—no man has talked them into any of that—I think that's part of the appeal."

"But aggression is not a part of our culture's definition of femininity." This was something they worried about in advertising a lot. "And I thought that you—I mean, most men like to be in control all the time."

Wiley came as close to grinning as Janet had ever seen him. "Not all the time."

"And I assume your knowledge of pornography comes entirely from First Amendment cases?"

"Absolutely. How could you think otherwise?"

Like a good boy, Wiley finished reading his rock and roll book the next day, and at dinner, the two of them discussed why he had liked it.

"Well, I enjoyed learning new things; a lot of that was entirely new to me, but it was presented so clearly I could follow it. And I especially liked the passages of things I could relate to, some of the contracts cases or when they were talking about a song I could remember—"

"Red M&M's."

"People can relate to red M&M's?"

"I can. I miss them. The orange ones just aren't the same."

Wiley laughed. "What a piteous life you lead. What other emotional deprivations do you suffer from?"

She could have told him, but this hardly seemed like the time to bring it up. She wasn't going to let the conversation drift off the subject.

That was such a problem for them. She responded to everything he said on a very personal level, while he was detached when they talked, not thinking about the personal. He had been joking a moment ago, and she had been about to take it seriously. No wonder they had trouble communicating.

Well, she could try to change.

"You're changing the subject," she said instead. "What else made you enjoy the book or not enjoy it?"

"I found some of the straight, flat history sections a little boring."

"The Anglo-Saxon land law parts?"

"What?" Then he remembered his outline. "Now, Janet, there are a lot of people who are interested in Anglo-Saxon land law."

"And I'm sure they're a real fun group, but why don't we forget about them? What else did you like?"

"Well." He paused. "I don't know . . . this is going to make me sound like a sap, but I think I was the most engrossed when it read like a novel— when you could understand the personalities of the people and how things happened because of the kind of people they all were. That was surprisingly interesting."

Well, of course, Janet wanted to say. How typical of Wiley to be surprised that he liked what everyone liked—the vignettes, the personalities, the gossip. But at least he admitted it, that was something. In the past, if some portion of his character seemed to be more like a human being than a perfect lawyer, he repressed it, ruthlessly stuffing it back into the pin-striped cage.

Janet spoke carefully. "Does a regulation ever get written for the wrong reason? Because of political reasons or because of the personalities involved?"

"All the time. I can think of any number of cases. Of course, we were involved with one of them so I can't—"

He stopped, but she knew what he was about to say—he couldn't write about a case he had worked on; it would be unethical.

"Well, then, don't write about those," she said. "Just try to find out if the reason we didn't have cranberries that year was that someone had the hots for someone else's wife—that's something people would be interested in."

Within a few days Wiley had written another outline. Each chapter was developed to a single point he wanted to make—how the rules were sometimes written for reasons that had little to do with the issues involved, how sometimes regulations had effects that no one could have imagined, things like that.

"But some of the examples sound like bar stories," he said.

"So?"

They were making dinner, a Szechwan chicken dish. They had already finished chopping everything, and Wiley was setting the table while Janet stir-fried the dish.

We haven't done anything like this in years, worked

in the kitchen together, not since before we were married, back in the group house.

And maybe they still weren't the ideal upscale, young professional couple who got written up in *The Washingtonian* magazine because they trained for marathons together, but Wiley and Janet were chopping scallions together. It was a start.

However, not a perfect start, Janet immediately realized. She had been paying more attention to her thoughts than to the recipe, and she dumped the soy sauce mixture in at the wrong time. She stared into the wok, wondering what to do about it.

"What's the problem?" he asked.

"Nothing." She started to stir-fry the broccoli even though it was swimming rather than sizzling. "I just screwed things up a bit, but it probably won't matter. We can always have tuna casserole."

"Or we could starve; I would almost prefer that." Wiley hated casseroles, especially those that started with Campbell's Cream of Mushroom soup. Fully a third of the recipes Janet had learned from her mother Wiley considered revoltingly Midwestern.

"At least we'd be doing it together," Janet said.

"I'm sure it would be very romantic." He took the plates out of the cupboard and put them on the counter next to her. "But speaking of doing things together..."

Janet was lifting the broccoli out of the wok. "Yes?"

"I'm a little concerned about my prose style. I'm afraid it will sound like a brief, and I'd appreciate it if you could read a draft. I hate to bother you—"

Wiley was asking for her help. He had never done that before. Never. People at work were always asking Janet for help, telling her that they needed her. But never Wiley. "You know I will," she breathed. "I'll be glad to help."

He smiled. "I thought you would. You generally do let people take advantage of you."

"You think I'm a sucker, don't you?"

"Yes. But for a sucker, you have an amazing prose style."

The wok fell back down on its rim with a clatter. "Wiley!"

"Oh, come on. You knew I thought that."

"I did not."

"Are you sure? I can't imagine that I wouldn't have mentioned it."

"I'm sure." She knew her prose was excellent; everyone at work knew it, but she didn't know that Wiley had known. "I wouldn't have forgotten that, believe me, I wouldn't have forgotten that."

His years at the firm had taught Wiley to work quickly, and it didn't take him long to produce the necessary two chapters. Janet rewrote them completely, making the sentences shorter, the verbs stronger, cutting most of the qualifying detail. "Your reader's not going to care about that."

But, to Wiley's mind, it wasn't accurate enough without all the qualifications and exceptions, so he put them back in.

The editor loved the proposal and sent back a

contract. He praised "Wiley's" prose and said that the only real problem was too much nitpicking detail.

"I guess he liked your way better than mine," Wiley said after reading the editorial letter.

"Advertising teaches you a lot about communication," she said mildly.

He looked blank for a moment as if this were a very new idea. "Yes," he said slowly, "yes, I guess it would."

Janet spent a lot of time working with Wiley on the book. She knew that in theory, she was giving more than he, that if their positions were reversed, he probably would not have tried so hard to help her. But last winter she had told herself if he would just take the first step toward improving their marriage, she would do anything. Well, he hadn't abandoned his profession in order to make things better with her, but writing this book was having that effect. They were spending time together; they had a common interest, a shared goal.

Work had been driving them apart; now at last it was bringing them together.

But if she weren't going to bring agency work home at night, if she were to leave as soon after five as she could, it meant spending her whole day planning campaigns with Alan or writing.

But people kept coming to her with administrative problems.

"Look," she finally told an account executive who was complaining about an ad for a health maintenance organization, "it's the art you don't like, not the copy. The Art Department is that way. Go bitch at Alan, not me.''

The young account exec looked surprised. "But we always bring problems to you. He's hard to deal with.''

"He's creative director. Even if it were the copy you didn't like, you should still take it to him.''

About an hour later Alan strolled into her office. She assumed that he had come to complain to her because the account exec had complained to him.

But he had something else on his mind.

"Where's the creative for the WALX pitch?'' he asked instead.

"What are you talking about?''

Alan sat down in one of the pale gray chairs and put his feet up on her glass conference table. "Wrong answer, Janet," he said calmly. "The right answer is 'In this folder here.' ''

"Were we doing creative for that?''

In general, when they tried to win a new account, they showed the prospective client ads that the agency had done in the past. Most of their accounts were too small to justify any more effort.

But for more lucrative accounts, advertising agencies did look at the client's product and put together concepts for TV, radio, and magazine ads, showing the client not just what they had done for other people in the past, but what they would do for him in the future. This was the only way to land a big account.

WALX was a big account, a new, well-financed radio station in Alexandria, another Virginia sub-

urb. When Janet, Michael, and Alan had decided
to go for the account, they had known they would
have to put together a creative package. But somehow Janet had forgotten about it, and obviously
Alan had too.

"We don't have a prayer without creative,"
Alan said unnecessarily.

"Then we don't have a prayer." Janet paged
through her calendar. "The meeting's tomorrow;
we might as well cancel."

"Nonsense. It's only noon. The meeting's not
until three tomorrow. We can do it; we've done
fire drills like this before."

It was tempting. Janet loved listening to the radio. That's what she wanted to do the campaign
about—the way the songs became a part of your
fantasies or what is was like when you had spent
the whole day hearing a song in your head and then
you would turn on the radio, and suddenly they
would play it, this song you had been hearing, and
it was like they knew what you had wanted to hear
and they were playing it just for you. She ached to
write an ad that would capture just that feeling.
Ideas were tumbling out of her.

"All right, Alan. Let's do it."

He stood up, his dark eyes dancing. "We'll kill
'em."

And suddenly it was like the old days again,
when they had first started to realize how good
they were. They were a team, working together,
their minds tripping over each other, leaping,
surging. At moments like these, Janet couldn't
imagine how two humans could be any closer.

Work . . . it was seductive, entincing, irresistible.

A few hours later she remembered to call Wiley to say that she wouldn't be home until very late.

"But this morning you said you'd be home by six."

Janet was instantly defensive. What nerve he had. How many times had he strolled in at ten o'clock without even calling? He had been doing this to her for years and years, and now she did it once, just once, and he acted like she had broken half the Commandments and three-quarters of the Girl Scout laws.

But before she could speak, he suddenly laughed. "Did I just sound like what I think I did?"

She softened, so glad that she hadn't spoken. If she'd been defensive, angry, he would have gotten distant and ironic. She should remember that. *Don't react so quickly all the time.*

"It's not a lot of fun," he went on, "being on the receiving end of this 'I'll-be-home-late,' is it?"

"Not in the least."

And Janet thought that that was a very useful piece of information for Wiley L. Hunt to acquire.

After the meeting the next afternoon Michael stopped by her office, trying to figure out what had happened the day before.

"I honestly don't know," she said. "It just fell through the cracks."

He picked up a folder and tapped it lightly on her desk so that the papers inside aligned themselves more neatly. "It was pretty important to be left to the last minute."

"I know that." Janet felt a little sick. For dinner

last night, she had had two Diet Pepsis, four cups of coffee, and about three hundred Pepperidge Farm Mint Milano cookies. For lunch today, she and Alan had shared a package of peanut butter crackers, a Milky Way bar, and a large bag of sour-cream-and-onion-flavored potato chips. And just when she had finally started to lose weight.

But she didn't just feel sick; she felt guilty too. "I'm sorry. I know we decided to do creative on this, but I just didn't schedule it, I don't know why. Maybe I thought Alan was going to follow through on it."

"Alan?" Michael raised his eyebrows. "Alan never follows through on anything if he can help it."

"I know that." She sighed. "But it does make things more difficult."

"We all manage to work around each other's foibles."

That was true. Everyone in the office was careful not to give Michael messy files or reports with coffee stains and dog-eared corners. And no one expected Alan to pay much attention to deadlines or budgets. It was all a part of working together.

Wait. No, it wasn't.

Sure, Michael was a bit weird about wanting everything neat, and it took a little extra time on everybody's part to cater to this. That was okay. That was a part of working together . . . especially when one half of the together is the boss.

But Alan not paying attention to deadlines and budgets, that wasn't a little foible.

Alan wasn't doing his job.

Alan was the creative director. Janet was the senior writer, and she knew what senior writers did. They wrote; they didn't schedule vacations, work out billing rates, approve expense accounts. Creative directors did.

Suddenly she sat up, her voice urgent. "Michael, I'm tired of doing Alan's job for him."

Michael leaned back in his chair. He didn't say anything.

"He's creative director, but I do everything that other creative directors do. I figure out assignments, I stand up to the clients, I fight with the account execs. That's all his job."

It had happened gradually, so gradually that she had hardly even realized it. Alan was exceedingly gifted, but he was no administrator. Janet had been running things since she was patrol leader in her Brownie troop. That's what the Girl Scout promise said—"To help other people at all times." So she'd helped Alan. And since she could do a lot of her writing at home at night, it had been easy to take care of these other matters during the day.

But she wanted her evenings back. Wiley needed her.

"Maybe you don't realize what has been going on," she continued, "but—"

"Oh, I know," Michael interrupted calmly. "You run the entire Creative Division, art as well as copy; you do it all. I know that."

"Why didn't you do something?"

"No one seemed unhappy about anything."

"But it wasn't right; it wasn't fair. I was doing Alan's job for him." She could hardly believe this; how could he have let this happen?

"Janet, I'm a businessman. If you were willing

to do a job without the salary, without the title, why on earth should I object?"

Janet stared at him, and he returned her gaze evenly. "Aren't you being naive?" he continued. "Don't expect that everyone is going to be fair just out of the goodness of their hearts. If you are going to let people exploit you, they will."

"You mean *you* will."

The accusation didn't bother Michael in the least. "Yes, I will. I'd do a hell of a lot to keep you here, Janet, but I won't do one thing more than I have to."

I'm a businessman. That's all she could think about on the way home, Michael saying "I'm a businessman." Michael and Alan were her friends—she'd always thought of them as her friends; that's why she'd been so willing to do things for them—but both of them had been using her.

Alan had the title, the salary, and the authority of creative director. He made more than she did; if they disagreed about an ad, ultimately she had to give way to him because he was creative director.

But all the bad parts of a creative director's job, all the tedious, vexing, time-wasting administration, all the things Alan hated to do, Janet did.

It was just like putting on the cord caulking with which they weather-stripped the windows of the condominium. Wiley hated doing it. Janet didn't mind. So every winter she did it. If one person hates to do something and the other one doesn't mind, then shouldn't the second person do it?

Her mother used to say that. "This won't be much fun, but it would be easier on us than on your grandmother, so we should do it."

Janet had lived her life that way; she was nice. Was that a mistake?

She was upset, depressed, she couldn't stop thinking about it, but as soon as she opened the door to the condominium, Wiley wanted to start talking about the book. "I think we're going to need to—"

"Not now," she snapped. "I just got home. At least let me change my clothes."

She brushed by him and went into the bedroom.

She barely had her blazer off when he came in. He sat down on the bed.

"Janet, I'm sorry," he apologized. "I know I used to come home from work with my head spinning, and of course, you must too. I didn't think, I'm sorry."

She looked over at him; her anger and irritation immediately dissolved. Being home was so hard on him. She had noticed that even now he would sometimes come out of the shower in the morning and automatically reach for a suit. Going to work each morning to a job he thought interesting and important had been the central thing he had understood about himself; being a good lawyer was what had, in his own eyes, made him a worthwhile human being.

Janet knew that he had to fight self-pity and self-doubt almost every day, but it was a battle he was winning. He wasn't absorbed in himself; instead he was learning from this experience. He was starting to understand other people's lives better. Including hers.

She went over and linked her arms around his neck. "I shouldn't bring work troubles home."

"It's inevitable." He leaned back, pulling her down with him until they were both lying on the bed. He rolled to his side. "Do you want to talk about it?"

He was looking down at her, his face interested and concerned. A year ago this would have never happened. He never thought her job was important enough to worry about. After all, it was only advertising.

But now his eyes looked so sympathetic that Janet felt it wouldn't have mattered what her job was. She could have been frying cheeseburgers behind a lunch counter and Wiley would have cared if her day had gone badly. He had never been like that before.

So she told him. "I'd never quite realized it before," she finished, "but I'm doing a lot more than my share."

He smiled. "Janet, you always do more than your share."

"But isn't that the right thing to do?"

"Not if it means that people are persistently taking advantage of you. I am sorry if this sounds like I am critizing you, but you keep thinking of your job as a friendship, where sometimes one person does more and then the other one does so that it all evens out in the long run. The rules of friendship are different from the rules of business."

And Janet had to admit that while she had been working for years, while she was successful and well-paid, she probably didn't know the first thing about the rules of business. Everyone she met in business she thought of as a potential friend. In her need to be friends with the entire world, she had probably been very, very unprofessional.

She could not just blame Alan and Michael for what had happened. She had allowed it.

"Rule and Champion are in business," Wiley said. "They want to make money off you, and you want to make money off them."

"I don't care about money," she said unhappily. No amount of money would ever stop her from feeling betrayed.

"With an unemployed husband, my dear, you'd better care about money. Anyway, it's money that's supposed to even it all out. If you're working harder than most senior writers, you shouldn't just be patted on the head for being such a nice person, you should be paid more than most senior writers."

He made it sound so simple, but that was such an alien way of thinking to her. "Are you saying that I should ask for more money?"

"In part. And you should decide if you want to be creative director."

"Creative dir—" She blinked. "But that's Alan's job, and he was one of the founders of the firm."

"But Michael owns sixty percent of it. What he says goes. So if you want to be creative director, tell him. Say that you'll leave otherwise."

"He'd never believe me. He knows I'd never leave. He knows how loyal I feel."

"And he takes advantage of that ... which is understandable. So tell him that I think you should leave. He'd believe me."

"Because you're both hardhearted."

"We're both realists, we know how to do business."

And Janet had to admit to him that if she ever did decide to start making demands at the agency, it would be easier that Michael and Wiley had never become chums.

"Did that bother you?" he asked. "That he and I weren't friends?"

"Yes. But then, of course, it made it easier to have an affair with him."

Wiley flinched. "Janet, I—"

"Wiley, I was teasing."

"I know. It's just that I so regret having ever said that to you. Do you understand that I never really thought it, that I knew you weren't the sort of woman who—"

She put her hand over his mouth. "You don't have to say it. I understand."

He kissed her fingers and then took her hand away. "I think it was the first time it ever occurred to me that I might lose you. And it bothered me."

"I should hope."

He laughed and Janet laced her fingers through his thick sun-streaked hair, pulling him down to her.

He kissed her, but then lifted his head. "Actually, speaking of your co-workers taking advantage of you, I suspect I am the worst offender here. You're working nearly as hard on this book as I am, and it would be an unpublishable mess if you weren't. I think we should list you as a co-author."

Janet sat up, surprised. Wiley wanted to give her credit for the work she was doing on his book. That surprised her. A lot.

But she shook her head. "No, I don't need public recognition." Any recognition that she needed she had just received. "This is one case where I think the rules of friendship do apply."

Chapter Eleven

"I had some interesting news today," Wiley said one evening during the next week.

"Oh?"

"One of the younger professors at Georgetown Law is leaving; he's going to work at Shadwell-Thompson."

Shadwell-Thompson was one of Hastings & Clark's competitors. Janet wasn't sure what this had to do with the two of them.

Unless...

"So his job is open?"

"It looks that way."

"Could you get it?"

"It's late enough in the year that not so many people will apply. It depends in part on how hard I try."

Which would, in turn, depend on how badly he wanted it.

Since he'd left Hastings & Clark, Wiley had only considered one job at all seriously. It had been with the general counsel's office of a large drug company. He would be responsible for helping the company conform to the many, many government regulations that it was subject to. It was work he was very well qualified for.

But whenever the company got sued, whenever it tried to change a regulation, whenever the legal work got interesting, they hired a firm like Hastings & Clark. Wiley would have been bored within six months. So he had turned it down.

And Janet was relieved. She longed for him to find a job that would make him happy, but the drug company had been in North Carolina. There wasn't much opportunity for her there.

"Would you like being in a law school?" she asked him now.

"I don't know," he admitted. "I've never really considered it because I liked being involved in things, in doing things that had day-to-day, practical consequences. Law professors have so little real power."

Janet shook her head. "I don't agree. Anyone who is teaching has a great deal of power. What a teacher does has enormous consequences."

"That's certainly true," he agreed.

Suddenly she was struck by how that interchange would have gone a month ago.

Oh, Wiley, how can you say that? she would have cried. *How can you say what teachers do isn't important?*

Stop being so sentimental, he would have snapped.

Her disagreement would have been phrased as an attack on him. "How can you say that?" And he would have attacked back.

How much better they were at communicating

now. Working together had taught them how to talk to each other.

And how much better still would things be if Wiley got a job at Georgetown. They would be in Washington. Their lives would be so much more normal than they had been when he was working at Hastings & Clark. Yes, a law professor worked very hard, occasionally even as hard as Hastings & Clark associates, but only occasionally. More important, a professor controlled his time. There wouldn't be this endless travel; there wouldn't be any more missed Christmases.

They could get a house and a—

She stopped herself. She shouldn't start fantasizing, not when it was all still so uncertain.

"I think you ought to try hard to get the job," she said. "You'll find out a lot about it in the interview process and you can always turn it down."

"I'll think about it."

Six months ago when Wiley said "I'll think about it" to any of Janet's advice, it meant he had already decided not to take it. Not anymore.

And in a day or so Wiley said he was going to submit a résumé.

The law school took their hiring very seriously, and Wiley spent a lot of time at the university, giving a lecture, attending seminars, having dinners. But the two of them still worked on the book.

One morning she got in to work late because she had started reading something over Wiley's shoulder and had lost track of the time. Michael called her, wanting to have lunch with her.

"You know," he said once they had ordered,

"the Creative Division over at WSN is pretty unhappy with their new management."

"Good heavens, Michael, I come late one day and you start talking about replacing me."

"As senior writer, yes."

"Michael!" She'd been joking. Goodness, he wasn't firing her, was he?

"Janet, you've made your point in the last few weeks."

"What point?" She hadn't been trying to make any point.

"We're in a mess when you just write. Alan's incapable of any kind of decent management."

"Oh." She hadn't been trying to prove that; she'd just been trying to spend more time with Wiley.

"So I guess we should try to woo Ted Silvers or Pam Houseman to be our senior writer and make you creative director."

Creative director. This was exactly what Wiley had said she should ask for. Did she want it?

Well, sure. She deserved it, didn't she? And Michael was right, they couldn't go on like this. They were growing so quickly; they kept getting bigger accounts; they were on the short list over at WALX; Alan could not be depended on.

"It's a perfect solution," Michael said. "Alan will fuss, but not a lot, I think. He's hated the last few weeks, having to deal with the things you've stopped taking care of. And you are so good at management, Janet; you really do deserve it. To say nothing of the fact that we need you."

"I guess I really don't have a lot of choice." She had to do this; they needed her.

"Of course you have a choice," Michael returned. "And I want you to think it over carefully"—he paused meaningfully—"because you couldn't continue this leaving at five thirty routine."

That was true. She'd have to work harder than she had ever worked before, even harder than she had worked while Wiley had been in Houston.

The agency needed her, but Wiley needed her. She did not know what to do.

And what about her own needs? This would be a promotion, more money, more authority, more prestige . . . and the end of all the Little House in the Big Suburbs fantasies.

"I don't know," she said slowly. "We'd fall apart if Alan—"

Michael shook his head. "No. Alan's down to art director, whatever you do. If you don't want to be creative director, then I'm going to start talking to Lou Laird."

Lou Laird was the creative director at WSN. "You'd bring him in over Alan and me?"

"I own sixty percent of the company," he said as an answer.

Janet twisted her diamond around on her finger. "I need to think about this."

"Of course."

"Champion certainly does play hardball, doesn't he?" Wiley said when he told her.

His voice was admiring.

"You understand, don't you," Janet said, "the position this puts me in? If I don't take the job, then Michael will bring in someone new, and that would spoil everything.''

Those long hours when she and Alan worked together, their powerful imaginations becoming one ... all that would change. Even if Lou Laird weren't in the room, he would always be a presence. They would have to worry about his taste, his judgment. They would have to please him. He would be their boss.

''Surely Michael's not going to hire someone who isn't very competent,'' Wiley said.

''Oh, no, I didn't mean that,'' she said quickly. ''Laird's work is super, he's the best.''

''Then what is it?''

She tried to explain. ''We're all so close there, and—''

''Janet, you aren't living in the *Mary Tyler Moore Show.* You don't have to be one big, happy family to get your work done.''

''Oh, Wiley.'' Janet felt tense, defensive. ''Why do—''

She stopped herself. *Don't react so quickly. First try to understand why you feel defensive.*

And the answer was easy.

Because he was right.

The people at the agency had been like a family, there was no doubt about it. Michael had been the daddy, quiet, a little distant, responsible for the money. She had been the mommy, bustling about, concerned about everybody's feelings, the one that people brought their troubles to, the one who would do what no one else was willing to. And Alan had been the indulged oldest son, a spoiled brat with great power because Mom and Dad were afraid of his temper tantrums.

Janet supposed that in many offices, people fell into such roles.

How pathetic it now seemed, a threadbare substitute for a real family, bringing very complex emotions into their place of business.

When Janet had lived in the group house her first year in Washington, she had thought it sad that the house was nearly all that some of the residents, including Wiley, had had for a family. She had enjoyed living there, but it had never been a substitute for her family.

But over the last few years, with her marriage so empty, she too had grafted on to a substitute family...and she hadn't even realized that it was happening.

Alan was insistent the next day. "I hope you aren't thinking about letting Michael talk to Laird."

"Alan, if you had been doing your job, this wouldn't have come up."

"But everything will be all right if you'll be the creative director." Clearly Alan was so worried about Laird coming that he wasn't bothered by Janet taking over his job.

"The agency is growing, Alan. We've got to change."

"But I like things the way they are. We're like a family—"

No. We work together, that's all. Wiley is my family. The two of us may not have children or a dog or a house, but we're still a family.

"Alan, it's crazy for me to take on a new job when Wiley's career is still unsettled."

"What difference does that make?"

"What do you think I'd do if he got a job outside Washington?"

He stared at her blankly. "You wouldn't leave, would you?"

"He's my husband."

"You'd leave us?" Alan seemed numb, disbelieving. "Just because he's changing jobs?"

He's just uncomfortable when it comes to Wiley. Janet remembered Alan saying that about Michael.

Well, of course. If they had been playing out these family roles, then Wiley was a threat to the family, the force that could disrupt the relationship between Janet and Alan.

Wiley had power, he could make demands, he was the man who had a right to Janet's time, her attention, her loyalty, rights that Alan secretly, subconsciously, felt to be his alone.

Oh, God, weren't things complicated enough without people dragging their Oedipal complexes into work with them?

Alan had known that she was married, but he had never had to confront what that meant—that, for her, there was a bond stronger than the one she felt for the agency, for their mock-family. Alan would feel threatened, defective, as if her commitment to Wiley were a judgment on Michael and himself, as if she were saying to them "You do not mean as much to me as he does."

Of course, they didn't mean as much to her as

Wiley did. But that Alan was disappointed, even surprised, just showed how close she had come to the reverse.

There had been a time when the people she had worked with did seem more deserving of her loyalty than her husband, but not anymore.

That evening Wiley was doing something at the law school, so Janet was having dinner with Mary Keane. They met at the same restaurant they had gone to right after Wiley had come back from the Caribbean.

"I'm going to have broiled fish and iced tea," Mary announced.

"That's easy for you," Janet returned. Mary was starting to seem happy again. She hadn't moved back home, but she was seeing Tim regularly, and she had been so outraged when George Landis had gone to the *Post* with the information about Wiley and FalCon that she hadn't seen him in nearly a month. "I'm going to have something with a thick, disgusting cream sauce. I deserve it."

"What's the problem?"

"I'm being promoted."

"Oh, my God, how awful." Mary craned her head, looking around the room. "Where are the M&M's? There's a major life tragedy going on; this person needs some sugar."

Janet explained everything to Mary, not just the creative directorship, but the family roles they had all been playing. "I feel very loyal to the agency, but . . . I don't know how it happened . . . but suddenly I feel like I am in the middle of a very sick situation where a group of people are trying to be everything to each other, friends, family, colleagues.''

"At least you aren't lovers."

"But if I hadn't been married, if I hadn't had at least that connection with the outside world, I probably would have gotten involved with one of them." Janet closed her eyes, almost faint at how claustrophobic, how incestuous, that would have been. "Thank God for Wiley."

"That's a nice way to feel about your husband," Mary said quietly.

"That's another thing about the job. Things have been wonderful the last month because I've been spending so much time with Wiley. I couldn't do it if I took the new job."

"But what if Wiley becomes Wiley again? What if he lands in some sort of job, in which all that ambition takes over again? What if next year suddenly becomes like last year, won't you regret not being creative director?"

"Maybe," Janet sighed, "but that's a risk I have to take. If I protect myself against that, then it just helps insure that it will happen."

"Do you worry that you are taking bigger risks than he is?"

"No. He took the first step. I'm perfectly willing to take the next five or six."

"You're downtrodden and exploited." Mary's voice was affectionate.

"Well, sure. But I'd rather be downtrodden and exploited by the man I love than the men I work for."

"That seems like a grim choice."

"It's not really."

The waiter approached them and Janet resolutely ordered fish and tea. She had just lost the weight she had gained during Wiley's job crisis when the crisis at her job had come up. It was a good thing this family only had two jobs. Otherwise she probably wouldn't be able to get up out of her chair. "I'm sorry," she would have to call in. "I'd really like to come in to work today, but I'm too fat to get through the door."

"All we've done is talk about me," Janet said after the waiter took their boring, but healthy order. "How are you?"

"Pretty good," Mary acknowledged. "I've decided to appear at my husband's side at that thing up in New York."

"What thing?"

"That retirement dinner for David Franklin."

"Do I know what we're talking about?"

"Of course you do. The Franklins are old friends of Wiley's parents."

"That's right. They gave us a sterling serving bowl for a wedding present; I almost never use it."

"Well, you can give it back to him as a retirement gift."

Although Tim Keane and Wiley had never met until they started working for Hastings & Clark, they were, in the way of a certain type of Northeasterner, linked by several connections. One of them was that David Franklin, an old friend of Lee Hunt, was Tim's godfather.

Franklin was retiring—or rather being retired—from his law firm, Mary said; there was a dinner for him in New York in a few weeks. Although the invitations weren't out, she was sure that Wiley knew about it. "Tim mentioned it to him."

"Well, he didn't mention it to me."

Janet asked Wiley about it that night.

"We'll be invited all right, but I don't see any reason to go. It'll just be a bunch of lawyers. You won't have a good time."

As much as Janet thought Wiley had grown a great deal more sensitive and thoughtful, she didn't for one minute believe that he was staying home because he cared whether or not she would have a good time. Three months ago he would not have missed this dinner, and his not wanting to go now said a lot.

Denial, anger, bargaining, depression, acceptance.

Wiley hadn't seemed depressed anymore. He was relaxed, open, warm, loving. But acceptance hadn't come yet.

To him, being at home writing the book was a holiday, a break. He knew perfectly well that he wasn't going to be a house husband forever, so he was happy to play at being the cook, the errand boy, because he knew himself only to be playing at it. It didn't threaten his self-image, it didn't depress him.

But what he still hadn't accepted was that he would never be an attorney with a major law firm again. That's why he didn't want to go to New York, that's why he didn't want to be at that retirement dinner. He didn't think he could face all those people who still were what he would never again be. He couldn't bear to be standing on the shoulder of the expressway, watching all the cars whip by.

Three months ago Janet would have told this to Alan or Michael. But not anymore. Now she was saying it to Wiley.

"Wiley, you can't go on avoiding people who work at big law firms."

He stiffened. "I'm not avoiding anyone."

They were in the bedroom. It was now a part of their routine that he came back and talked to her while she changed out of her work clothes.

She sat down next to him on the bed. "There's no reason why you should be feeling like a failure. You're writing an interesting book that's going to change the way a lot of people think; you're interviewing for a teaching job." *You've taken a marriage that was empty, that was pointless, and made it matter again.* "There's nothing to be ashamed of."

"I'm not ashamed."

"Then why are you cutting yourself off from people you've known for years and years?"

"I'm not cutting myself off; I'm just busy, that's all. And anyway, I think it will be on our anniversary."

Their wedding anniversary had never been sacred. Wiley had been out of town several years. This had always disappointed Janet. Her parents thought their anniversary was more important than either of their birthdays.

"We could spend the weekend in New York," she said. "That would be a celebration. We can get tickets for something."

"I thought you didn't like New York."

That was true. "I like being with you," she answered honestly.

She doubted that what she had said would make any difference to him, but when the invitation did come, Wiley stared at it. "Well, I guess we can go if that's what you want."

Chapter Twelve

Janet turned down the creative directorship, and in the end, after hours and hours of thought, it seemed like an easy decision.

She wasn't particularly ambitious; she didn't care much about money; she certainly wasn't eager to take on more administrative responsibilities. Had she taken the job, it would have been because people had asked her to, because she felt like they needed her to.

She knew that part of her reaction came from the mother role that she played at the agency. It was if Michael had been saying "There's simply no one else to lead the Brownie troop; there won't be a Brownie troop if you don't lead it, and all the little girls won't get to sell cookies and make sit-upons."

Janet could have never said no to that. She would have lead the Brownie troop.

But this was different. What Michael was really saying was "There's simply no one else as *cheap* as you." He was going to have to pay Lou Laird a third more than he would have had to pay her.

This was a professional proposition. She could say no to it . . . and she did.

Nonetheless, when Alan brushed by her in the hall without speaking, she felt terrible.

Any mother would.

She told Wiley so that night.

"Janet, there's no reason for you to feel guilty that you are turning down a job."

"I know," she sighed. But it was so hard to shake old habits; whenever anyone had asked for volunteers, she and her sisters had always put their hands up first. ·

"If you want to feel guilty about something," he said, "we could go to Baskin-Robbins after dinner."

Ice cream always made Janet feel very guilty.

"You're a big help," she told him.

"Thank you. I try. Now, where shall we go to eat? What about the Thai place?"

"Oh." Janet suddenly felt a little guilty again. "I was going to make dinner."

"You were? Why? You haven't made dinner in weeks. You don't need to, let's go out. If you want to eat here, I can pick up a carryout."

"Well..."

Janet knew what she was doing. Here she had felt guilty about turning down a more demanding job so she had to run home and be Betty Crocker.

She knew what the ads had to say, she had even written some of them: A good wife, a good mother, spends hours in the kitchen. Food was how a woman showed her family that she loved them.

But Janet was being a better wife than she had ever been in her life. She wasn't doing Wiley's laundry, she wasn't cooking at all—he was doing all that—but she was meeting his other needs, his intellectual, emotional, and psychological needs, better than she ever had, even better than during the first year she had known him, when he was mourning his mother.

"Thai it is," she said briskly. "And let's eat there. I don't even want to have to throw out the trash."

After they ordered, Janet asked him what great things had happened to him during the day.

"Well, actually—" He paused. "It's odd timing that it happened on the day you turned down a promotion, but ..."

"But what? Did Georgetown call?"

He nodded.

"Oh, Wiley, did they?" She was thrilled. "Did they offer you the job?"

"Not officially, but they are gearing up the paperwork."

It was going to happen; it was actually going to happen. Things were going to work out for them. Wiley had found a new job—and not just a job, but a career, something he could really care about.

It would be perfect, both of them would have jobs they liked, jobs they found interesting, but the jobs wouldn't be everything; they would still have a life.

But Wiley wasn't saying anything. His head was turned sideways, away from her. He was staring blankly across the room, and in a moment, he started to rub the back of his neck.

"You want this, don't you?" she asked urgently. "It does make you happy too, doesn't it? I won't be happy if you aren't."

"I guess it's what I want."

But he sounded tired again, just like he had before.

It takes time, Janet told herself. *It's only June. He left Hastings & Clark in April. He hasn't accepted it all yet. But he will.*

Janet called Mary the next morning to tell her about these family career developments, but Mary had, according to her secretary, called in sick.

"Mary? Sick?" Janet was surprised.

"It is a shock," the secretary agreed. "Not that she's sick, but that she didn't come in. Nobody takes sick leave around here. They just drag their aching, contagious bodies in and spread their germs around. The entire outfit has a cold and the flu from October to March."

Janet smiled as she hung up. The agency was like that.

But no longer. The new Janet, plain old senior writer Janet, was going to stay home when she was sick. Mothers can't take sick leave, but senior writers could.

Janet thought about calling Mary at home, but didn't want to wake her up if she was sleeping.

About an hour later Janet's secretary, Kris, buzzed her, saying that Mary was calling.

Janet picked up the phone. "Mary, what a woman of great, good sense you are."

Mary did not answer. Not a word.

"About taking sick leave," Janet said, suddenly awkward. "I mean, I thought workaholics never took sick leave, that they just got—"

"Uh, Janet, I'm across the street, at the coffee shop. Do you think you could get away?"

Across the street? Janet was instantly concerned. Mary was in a coffee shop in the middle of the morning? How very unlike her. Mary was much more than sick. Something must be wrong, terribly wrong.

"I'll be right down," Janet said instantly.

She seized her purse and told her secretary that something had come up and she didn't know when she would be back. She stuck her head in Michael's office and repeated the same message.

Alan was there. "Is this the kind of behavior we can expect of you from now on?"

She didn't answer him, but yes, yes, it was.

Oh, she wouldn't shirk her responsibilities. Undoubtedly she was going to continue to do much, much more than her share. But there were limits now.

She remembered the week Wiley had come back from the Caribbean. She had hoped to get in a little shopping before meeting Mary for dinner, but when Michael came into her office, she had immediately abandoned the idea of shopping. She thought of herself as a person who would drop anything when a friend needed her.

But she had been wrong about herself. She would drop anything except *work*, and increasingly she had done so only when the people at *work* had needed her. That's why it had been so long since she had seen Ellen and Terry, Jody and Bobbi, all her old friends. She hadn't had time for them.

That was going to change.

She was across the street in a few minutes. Mary was sitting in the back booth, facing away from the door. In a moment Janet saw why— Mary had been crying.

Janet had never seen Mary cry.

She sank down across from her. "Mary, what is it?" Mary's hand was cold.

"Nothing much. Just that my whole life is falling apart, that's all."

"But ... I thought—"

"That everything was going great? Well, it was and then ... Oh, God, why me?" Mary covered her face with her hands.

Janet reached across the table again and touched her arm. "Tell me."

It took Mary a moment, and when she lifted her head, her eyes were defiant. "I just got back from a little session at our friendly neighborhood abortion clinic."

Friendly neighborhood abor—"Mary!"

"Yes, it was some interesting experience, not one that I would recommend."

An abortion? Mary had had an abortion? "Why didn't you call me?" Janet gasped. Mary must have been alone, surely even a Hastings & Clark associate wouldn't drop his wife off at a coffee shop twenty minutes after she had had an abortion. Surely not. "I would have gone with you."

"No, I thought it would be easier if I didn't say anything to anyone, just went, had it taken care of, and that would be that."

Janet shook her head. "Oh, Mary, I'm sure it wasn't that easy."

"Well, I wouldn't know." Mary's laugh was short. "I didn't go through with it."

Janet hadn't realized she'd been holding her breath. "What happened?"

"I showed up and gave them my name like a

good little girl. They told me to sit down and I did. And, I don't know, Janet, maybe it was that the lights were so bright that they bothered my eyes, but I just started crying, and I couldn't stop. I could have been you, sitting there. I mean, I never cry, just never, but there I was, weeping away, like what's-her-name in that myth, the weeping stone—"

"Niobe," Janet said automatically. "What happened then?"

"Oh, the nurses, the counselors, all clustered around and tried to talk to me, but, of course, they have this policy against performing abortions on sprinkler systems, which struck me as reasonably sensible."

"Mary, start at the beginning. Where was Tim? Why wasn't he with you?"

"Tim? As in Tim Keane? My occasional husband? I didn't tell Tim, my dear, because I'm not sure this baby is his."

"Mary! But I thought—"

"That I'm not seeing George anymore? That's right, I'm not now, I've only seen him once or twice since he told the *Post* about Wiley, but I may have 'seen' George just once too often."

Janet did not know what to say.

"You know," Mary continued, "back before he met me, when he was dating around, Tim said he used to get his American Express bill and have to pay for dinners when he hadn't seen the woman he had taken for weeks. Well, in this case, it's a little more than an American Express bill hanging around."

"Mary, don't joke. We can talk seriously about this."

Apparently Mary couldn't because she went on in the same vein. "You know how grocers always put the new lettuce at the back of the bin so that customers will take the old stuff first? Well, that is a good policy for lots of things, including contraceptive products. I mean, I've been buying that jelly for years, and I'd keep putting the new tubes in the front of the shelf and when I needed one, I'd take out the tube on the front. When I moved my stuff out of our—Tim's place, everything got nicely jumbled up and I quite cheerily started using some that had expired years ago. It never occurred to me to check. And if that wasn't bad enough luck, I managed to do it during the month that I stopped sleeping with George and started sleeping with Tim again. Isn't that lovely? Doesn't this sound like a soap opera?" Suddenly Mary stopped, her brittle tone fading. "Oh, Janet, what kind of woman doesn't know who has gotten her pregnant?"

Janet wasn't sure how to answer that. Mary was thinking of herself as a tramp, a whore. *What kind of woman doesn't know who has gotten her pregnant?*

But she wasn't an evil person. Yes, she had done something very foolish, very wrong, but she was Janet's friend, and Janet loved her.

Janet took a breath. Maybe this was the time to take a page out of Wiley's perfect-lawyer book and to act very calmly. "When did you last sleep with George? How far along in your cycle were you?" she asked as mildly as Wiley would have.

"I guess my period had been over for a day or so."

"And when did you start sleeping with Tim?"

"Oh, God, I don't remember . . . I guess it was after the Douglas case settled so it must have been on the nineteenth."

Janet pulled a calendar out of her purse and did the sort of figuring that surprisingly Mary had not done. The nineteenth was ten days after she'd slept with George, day sixteen of her cycle. Sixteen wasn't as good as fourteen, but the baby was almost certainly Tim's.

"Then, Mary—" Janet stopped. What was the point? If Mary had been willing to listen to evidence like this, she would have done all these calculations herself.

Indeed Mary was looking for reasons to expect the worst. "None of those dates mean anything. I'd just gone on a diet . . . I was getting a little panicked about me and my swimming suit . . . and diets always mess me up, that's why it took me so long to get worried about my period being late."

Before Janet could answer, a tired-looking waitress shoved two tattered menus across the Formica table. "Coffee, hon?" she asked Janet. Mary already had a cup.

Janet opened the menu, suddenly craving something sweet. But then she closed it. "Yes, just coffee."

Mary was punishing herself. Guilty over her affair with George, she was looking for a scarlet letter to wear. Not until she had resolved those feelings would she be reassured by the evidence of the calendar, by the difference between day six and day sixteen.

"Now, Mary—"

Mary interrupted. "So I just thought I'd go get an abortion and not tell anyone. I mean, Janet, I don't feel pregnant. I don't feel the least bit different, not radiant, glowing, or nauseated. I feel fine, just like myself. That's why I assumed an abortion would be easy because this just doesn't seem real."

"But it is real." Yet Janet couldn't quite believe it either. Mary was pregnant.

"I guess a part of me knows that." Mary sighed. "Knows that this is a baby and all...but that sounds so strange, me with a baby, I just can't imagine it."

Of course. A surprise pregnancy would be hard on Mary even if she had been the perfectly faithful wife. She wouldn't be as miserably guilty, but she would still be uncertain. Motherhood had never been in Mary's plans. She didn't dislike children, but she knew nothing about them.

"There are other options, Mary," Janet said quietly. "You can have the baby and give it to adoptive parents—there are people out there who would bless you every day of their lives if you did—or you change your image of yourself. You can start thinking of yourself as someone who can bring up a child."

"Me? Are you kidding?" Mary asked. "Remember, I'm the one who said I was afraid of intimacy. I mean, this is intimacy city here. Some stranger has taken up residence in my body. How would you like that?"

I'd love it.

"Seriously, though," Mary continued, "I've never thought of myself as having children. I mean, I never even thought I'd get married. I always said that, that I'd never get married, not after I saw what being married did to my mother."

Janet knew nothing at all about Mary's mother; Mary never talked about her family. "But you did get married."

"And look where it's gotten me."

"Just because you've never thought of yourself as doing something doesn't mean that you can't do it. Wiley never thought he'd leave the firm. He's having to change his image of himself."

Mary saw the parallel. "Has he accepted it? Does he think of himself as a professor now?"

"Not entirely," Janet said, "but he's getting there."

"But he had you."

"And you have Tim."

"Oh, sure. Don't forget, Janet, we don't know who this kid's father is."

"Maybe Tim can accept that."

Mary shook her head. "How could he? How could any man? And I don't want to put anyone through what I went through with my father."

Janet looked up, curious.

"Oh—" Mary was suddenly evasive. "He kept doing an on-again, off-again number, and..."

Clearly she didn't want to talk about her own father and so Janet went back to talking about Tim. "You don't know what he'll say. That's one thing Wiley and I learned working on this book. You can't be second-guessing each other all the time, trying to communicate by guessing what the other person will say in advance of his saying it. We used to do that continually, and now you are doing it to Tim. Give him a chance. At a minimum, he can try to sue the drug company for not putting the expiration date on a bigger label."

"Hastings & Clark? Sue a drug company? Surely you jest."

"You're right. Well, then, he could sue the FDA for not forcing the drug company to use bigger labels."

"That's more like it."

Janet did not go back to work that day. "Are you sure you shouldn't go back?" Mary kept asking.

"They'll survive without me."

"See, you aren't a classic workaholic. The true CW believes he is indispensable."

"I believe I'm indispensable." Janet defended her right to be considered pathological. "At the moment, you'd go bonkers without me."

"Well, that's certainly true."

That night Janet told Wiley what had happened.

He whistled. "That's one tough situation."

"Yes, it is, but it's probably not as awful as she thinks." Janet explained about the timing and the dates. "She's stuck on the fact that she deserves to be miserable, so she's determined to believe that the baby isn't Tim's."

"But aren't blood tests pretty sophisticated now?" Wiley asked.

"Yes, but she needs to sort through all these feelings long before the baby is born. Tim does too. Mary won't want some kind of conditional commitment from him, 'Let's live happily ever after if the baby looks like me.' That's no basis for the marriage.''

"And babies never look like anyone to me," Wiley said. "When people are clucking around saying that so-and-so looks exactly like one of the parents, I can never see the resemblance. This one would have to come out wearing a pair of horn-rimmed glasses for me to think it looked like Tim." Then he sobered. "I wonder how I'd feel."

Janet wondered too. How would he feel if this were happening to her? Thank God it wasn't. "Well, you're in luck. Michael's had a vasectomy." Janet had no reason in the world to think such a thing. "So I didn't have to worry when I was with him."

"Janet . . ."

"Oh, come on," she said lightly. "That's the worst thing you've ever said to me. I insist on the right to tease you about it for the rest of your life." She stood up. "What shall we do about dinner?"

Wiley took her hand, pulling her back down to the love seat. He was still serious. "It may have been the worst thing I've ever said to you, but it's not the worst thing I've ever done. I was just as bad a husband during the U.S. Oil case as Tim was."

"I know that."

"So why didn't you do what Mary did?"

"I don't know," she answered honestly. "I wanted to hurt you just as much as Mary wanted to hurt Tim, but I guess my background gave me stronger support systems than Mary's gave her. I mean, my Sunday school had us memorizing the Ten Commandments long before I knew what the word 'adultery' meant.''

''It doesn't seem fair.'' Wiley got up and went over to the windows. The curtains were still open to the soft summer light. ''Here Dan, Tim, and I behaved in exactly the same way, and they are paying for it, and I'm not.''

Janet went over to him, slipped her arms around his waist, and pressed her cheek against his back. He was wearing another rugby shirt. The cotton was soft.

She could hardly believe what she had heard. Dan and Tim still worked at Hastings & Clark, but in at least one way, Wiley thought himself more fortunate than them.

''You know, Wiley,'' she admitted suddenly, ''you were right to be worried about Michael. Not sexually, there was never a sexual threat, but Michael and Alan both were a problem in our marriage. I felt closer to the two of them than I did to you. I confided in them, I told them my troubles instead of telling you. I think that that's as much of a danger as some quick roll in the hay.''

He nodded in agreement. ''You hear that about policemen, at least those who ride in squad cars all day, that they know their partner much better than they do their families, and it's a problem that doesn't have a thing to do with sex.''

Janet was disappointed that he had switched to a more general topic. That was what he used to do all the time; she would want to talk about themselves, he would want to talk about society at large.

But he went on. "And that's what it seemed like during the U.S. Oil case, that we all knew what a once-in-a-lifetime opportunity it was, but that there wasn't a chance that any of you back here could understand how we felt, so none of us even tried to explain."

"It would have helped if you would have talked to me. It wouldn't have been enough, but it would have helped."

"I know," he admitted. "I was wrong."

"We came very close to ruining our marriage," she said.

"I know that too."

Just as they were sitting down to dinner, their doorbell rang.

It was Tim.

"Come in," Wiley said. "You're in luck tonight; Janet made dinner, not me."

Tim started to answer, then stopped.

Mary must have told him, Janet thought. He was a perfect lawyer. He always had the perfect, polished response. Not now.

"Tim, we know," she said suddenly.

His face was blank and he didn't move, except to slump against the doorjamb. "I know you do."

"Well, at least come in," Wiley said. "We don't have to talk about it with you out in the hall."

Tim insisted that Janet and Wiley return to their meal. He said he wasn't hungry.

Although he knew that Mary had talked to Janet, Tim still, as people in such circumstances always do, told them everything anyway.

"Do you want her to have an abortion?" Wiley asked bluntly.

Tim shook his head. "No, I guess I was an altar boy once too often to be comfortable with abortion ... especially the idea of Mary having one. And anyway," he continued, "in lots of ways I'm just as much to blame as she is. I mean, I know Mary, I know how insecure she is about some things. I know what her needs are, and I ignored them. If I had been more of a husband, she would have never had a thing to do with Landis." He sighed and shook his head. "Why did this have to happen? I really do love her, you know; I have wanted us to be back together for months."

"Even though she's had an affair?" Wiley asked.

"That's right."

Janet was surprised that Wiley had said anything. This was the sort of deeply personal conversation he usually avoided.

But he continued. "Then it's not fair to act like you've forgiven her for the act—that she slept with Landis—and then balk at the consequences—that she's pregnant."

"Am I being hypocritical?"

"Not really," Janet answered. "Wiley's right in theory, but in practice, it's a lot easier to forgive the things you can forget, and Mary being pregnant makes this a lot harder to forget."

"Well, you're right there," Tim agreed, "and that's what Mary's so worried about. She's convinced that I'll never be able to forget, and that it will be like her childhood all over again."

"Her childhood?" Wiley asked. "I don't think

I know anything about her childhood. Did she have problems with her parents?''

"No, just with her father. I guess her folks had to get married, but her father never really accepted it. Half of him wanted family life; the other half didn't. So for years, until she was six or seven, her father kept drifting in and out of her life, never really committing himself. He'd show up for a few weeks, she'd think they were going to be a normal family like everyone else, and then, poof, he'd be gone. This left her thinking that a child is better off with no father than half of one."

"Have you talked to Dan recently?" Wiley asked suddenly.

Tim looked a little surprised at the change in subject. "No, not really. Things aren't going so well for him at the firm—he's not concentrating—and I think he's avoiding me."

Janet could understand why Dan Stewart might be having trouble concentrating. His wife, Sarah, had filed for divorce and, worse, had announced a few days ago that she was moving to California.

Wiley was telling this to Tim. "It means that Dan is hardly ever going to see the baby. He says he doesn't see how he can be a father at all."

Tim was shaking his head. "I thought this was all supposed to be simple. I mean, my dad was just my dad. There wasn't any question about it. When did everything get so complicated?" He sounded bewildered. "I have to decide whether or not to be someone's father. What kind of decision is that?"

"Life has surprises," Wiley pointed out.

"Mine wasn't supposed to," Tim grumbled.

"Mine wasn't either."

Wiley's voice was quiet. Tim stopped fidgeting with the salt shaker and looked at his former colleague. At last he spoke. "I'm not used to this yet, but I guess it will be a whole lot easier than what you had to get used to."

Chapter Thirteen

When Tim left that night, Janet was sure that he had resolved to try to accept what had happened. But only a day or so later, he had to leave town. This time he went to Dallas.

"Does the state of Texas have it in for me or what?" Mary complained. "Here I am, one poor, defenseless pregnant woman, and that entire state is ganging up to ruin my life."

"When does he get back?" Janet asked.

"Probably never. He's going straight to New York for that retirement dinner."

"Aren't you going up for that? I am."

"I don't want to," Mary sighed, "but I suppose I will."

"Then let's travel together. Wiley's going up a couple days early to do some research."

"Okay," Mary agreed. "At least you'll be able to keep me from doing an Anna Karenina number in the path of a speeding train."

But on Thursday, Mary phoned to say that Tim was finishing up in Dallas earlier than he expected and had called, asking Mary if she would come to

New York Friday morning so they could spend the day together. "I'm going to take the Eastern shuttle," she told Janet. "It's harder to pitch yourself in the path of an airplane."

So on Saturday morning, Janet set off for New York alone.

She didn't like New York. Left to her own devices, she would never go up. She never knew where she was when she was there; she thought the city dirty, the people rude; she couldn't ever remember if she was supposed to be afraid of Central Park. Fortunately, Alan Rule liked Manhattan so much that he took care of all their New York business. She wondered if that would change when Lou Laird took over as creative director, if Lou would still let him go up twice a month. Oh, well, that was Alan's problem, not hers.

Janet was taking a Metroliner train. Wiley had suggested it, saying that he could come meet her if she came into Penn Station. She appreciated that. She was entirely capable of fending for herself, but she was just as happy not to.

He also insisted that she travel first class, which made no sense to her. True, the seats were slightly more comfortable and she'd get lunch, but it was only a three-hour trip, and the food would resemble airline food, the eating of which did not rank as one of the major thrills of even Janet's life.

But she did as she was told and settled obediently into her first-class seat.

"Are you Mrs. Hunt?"

She looked up at the uniformed, grizzle-haired

porter leaning over the aisle seat, smiling at her. "Yes, I am."

"Then these are for you." He handed her a square white florist box.

"They are?"

"Yes, ma'am." He smiled at her, a warm, grandfatherly smile. "I don't recollect having flowers delivered to a train since Amtrak took over."

He smiled again and for a moment, Janet thought he was going to pat her on the head and call her "Missy." She wouldn't have minded. But he moved away, and Janet was left alone with her flowers.

Gingerly she opened the white box. A delicate spray of lilies of the valley were caught with a jade green ribbon. The card read "Happy Anniversary, Wiley."

What a lovely gesture. When he was dreading the dinner with all those successful lawyers, when he was still struggling with his final reluctance to take the law school job, he had thought of her.

He was waiting for her when the train got into New York.

"Happy Anniversary," he said again, kissing her cheek.

She used to hate it when he kissed her cheek, it seemed so impersonal, but she hadn't then understood the kind of constraints he had grown up with. Her family was always touching one another, hugging, elbowing, tickling; his family never did. It had taken her a long time to understand that what would be formal and reserved in her was affectionate in him. And now she thought a kiss on the cheek was just fine.

She smiled up at him. "Thank you for the flowers." She touched the blossoms now pinned to the lapel of her white linen jacket.

"Did you like them?"

"You know I did. I felt like such a celebrity. But how did you arrange it?"

"It wasn't easy," he admitted. "That's why you had to come first class, but I found a florist whose father used to deliver huge bouquets of roses to Union Station back in the twenties and thirties. He got all nostalgic."

"So did the porter who delivered them."

"I suppose you cried." Wiley sighed.

"Of course. But I also remembered to tip the porter." Janet did not feel compelled to mention that it took her two and a half hours to remember to tip the porter.

"Good for you. You're on your way to being a certified grown-up."

"That is not necessarily one of the goals of my life," she pointed out.

Wiley laughed and picked up her bag and they passed through the station, up the escalators, and out into the street. A taxicab instantly stopped for them, something that never happened to Janet when she was up in New York alone.

They were, naturally, staying with Wiley's father. Janet opened her suitcase on one of the two twin beds back in the room Wiley had had through his adolescence and started to unpack.

Her own bedroom in Mint City had a double bed in it. Her parents had put one in when she got married. It was ironic, she thought, that it should be that way, a double bed out there, twin beds here. She felt very strange about making love in her old bedroom—it felt wrong somehow; her Pep Club letter still hung on the bulletin board next to the aged remains of her senior prom corsage.

She hung a blouse in the closet and turned back to him. "Do you think I'm weird?"

"Probably," Wiley answered immediately. "But in what context? It seems to me that anyone who is standing in front of his complete collection of Tom Swift books ought to be careful about who he calls weird."

"I'm talking about sex. Do you think I'm weird sexually?"

Wiley choked. "Janet, I don't think you need worry. No one could ever accuse you of being weird sexually."

"That's what I mean. Am I not weird enough? Am I a prude?"

He sat down on one of the beds and took her hand, pulling her down next to him. "What brought this on? Surely it wasn't what happened to Mary? How can you think that makes you look like a prude?"

"Oh, no," she said swiftly. "Not at all. It's being here. You don't mind making love here, but it bothers me to make love when we're in Missouri."

"I know it does. And I can understand."

"Does it bother you?"

He paused. "Do you want the truth?"

"Yes." Six months ago Wiley would have lied rather than hurt her feelings; she would have known that he was lying, which would have made her defensive.

"Well, sometimes it does. That bed is a lot smaller than what we're used to and you always seem so close and warm that sometimes I really want to, and it's not easy—"

Janet must have looked guilty, for he immediately spoke more lightly. "But, most of the time if the whole family's there, with your brothers and sisters upstairs with us, and we can hear people talking and doors closing and water running, I'm perfectly happy not to."

She appreciated his saying that. "I'm glad you don't think I'm a prude. I can live with the rest of the world thinking that as long as you don't."

He started to say something, then stopped.

"What is it?" she asked. "Are there some things you'd like to do that we haven't done?"

"Some," he admitted.

"Why didn't you tell me?"

"I didn't want to pressure you. I'd much rather go without something I want than do anything that makes you uncomfortable."

How nice he was. She'd never given him credit for being nice. He'd call it being "decent" or "only sporting," but it came out the same. "Well, maybe you should have at least given me a chance. I bet a lot are things that I just haven't thought about."

"You might be right. What's that thing you wear beneath your blouse?"

She wondered why he was changing the subject. "A camisole?"

"Whatever. Would you feel strange about leaving that on once in a while?"

She blinked. "Good Lord, no. Why should that bother me?"

"I don't know. I just thought it would so I never suggested it."

"You were second-guessing me."

He nodded, agreeing, apologizing. "Yes, I was."

"Maybe we ought to draw up lists," she said. "One thing from Column A would substitute for two things from Column B."

"Or maybe we could just show each other."

"That does sound a little more romantic," she admitted. She moved over closer to him. "Can anything in your Column A be done in a twin bed?"

"That does leave out Jell-O wrestling."

"Jell-O wrestling?"

"Absolutely. You'll love it. We can use red Jell-O if that would make you happy. Or even diet red Jell-O."

"Well, in that case ..."

Wiley gently tugged her back onto the bed, and the world was lost for the sake of his touch. She knew of nothing except his hands, his mouth, the familiar, loved shape of his body.

At least nothing until the phone rang.

"I'd better get that," Wiley groaned. "It might be Dad, changing plans."

"He probably has to work later than he planned," Janet said. And because she was a person of delicacy and refinement, she waited until Wiley was out of the room before adding, "Like father, like son."

In a moment Wiley came back. "That was Tim. He wanted to know if we want to meet them for a drink before the dinner."

It was already almost four. "I couldn't say no," he added.

"No, of course not. But we'd better get changed and go."

Janet had a momentary regret for Column A, which would now have to be postponed.

No, it's all right, she told herself. From now on, she and Wiley would have time. They would leave work at five like normal people, they would come home and spend the evening together. There would be plenty of time for Column A.

She stood up and started to unbutton her blouse. Or rather started to finish unbuttoning it.

She knew people who actually scheduled time for their spouses, writing it down on their calendars. Sex was a very structured thing for them, something that was bracketed, linked more to events and opportunities than to desire, happening on birthdays, anniversaries, weekends away, or when the children were sleeping over at someone's house.

But it wasn't going to be like that for them. If Tim and Mary needed them tonight, they would go. They could be alone some other time. From now on, she and Wiley would have plenty of time.

Janet's dress was a soft warm apricot. The fabric was silk and the dress floated as she moved. She started to fasten her emerald around her neck.

"Wait a minute," Wiley said. "I've got something for you. A sort of anniversary present."

He opened a drawer and took out a flat box,

wrapped in white paper with a design of tiny red shells and tied with a thin red ribbon, the kind that curled when pulled over a scissors blade, except on this package the ribbon was tied into a regular bow.

"You wrapped this yourself!"

"You can tell?" Wiley looked disappointed. "I knew I wasn't getting that bow right."

Janet wasn't disappointed at all. She couldn't care less if the bow was wrong. Wiley had never wrapped a present for her before. If the store wouldn't wrap it—or if he didn't have time to wait for the store to wrap it, which was more likely, since Wiley never shopped in stores that were too cheap to wrap things—she got her present unwrapped. Her thirtieth-birthday emerald hadn't been wrapped.

The thought of him standing in the drugstore, choosing between white paper with red shells and peach paper with aqua umbrellas...

"Oh, come on, Janet," he groaned. "You can't cry now. You haven't even opened the thing."

She fingered the package. Through the paper, she could feel the soft squish of a velvet jewelry case. Even if it was another quickly purchased, expensive piece, it would be different than her emerald. This one he had wrapped himself. Wiley was starting to spend time on her. That mattered more to her than his money.

The case looked slightly worn, which surprised Janet. She eased it open.

There on white satin lay a set of opals, a pendant, earrings, and a bracelet, the pale warm stones set in a soft rose gold.

She stared at them. She'd seen them before. Wiley's slim fingers reached into the case, lifting the pendant by the chain. "They were my mother's," he said.

He took the case from her and fastened the pendant around her neck and turned her to face the mirror so she could see how the warm colors in the stone's depth swirled and sparkled against the apricot of her dress.

"Okay, now you can cry."

Tim and Mary were waiting for them in the bar of the club where the dinner was to be held. Tim stood up.

"Don't you look lovely," he said to Janet as they came near.

"This old rag?" Wiley trilled. "Why, I just threw it on."

"Wait a minute," Tim protested. "You can't call that suit an old rag; I've got one just like that."

"My point exactly," Wiley returned in more normal tones.

Janet marveled at them. Wiley had been quiet in the taxi; he was dreading this evening, and Tim wasn't exactly on top of the world, but they were both hiding their feelings completely. They could clown with each other, they could have made small talk with strangers, they could have talked law with colleagues, and no one would have known how miserable they truly were.

"How are you?" Wiley asked Mary as he sat down.

"Great. I've thrown up three times this week."

Janet laughed. "I've always thought that morning sickness was a sign that human evolution wasn't complete. Even though we can walk upright and don't have ape hair on our backs, we've still got something to work on."

"I would much rather have ape hair on my back," Mary said instantly.

The rest of the conversation continued like this, light, amusing, slightly brittle.

"Are you guys okay?" Janet asked Mary as they stopped in the ladies' room before going upstairs to where the banquet was held.

"I think so. We're both trying hard, and that's a little wearing."

Janet thought of how hard she had tried all spring to learn how to communicate with Wiley. It had been very wearing. But worth it.

The banquet began with a cocktail hour, a hundred or so people mingling, slipping in and out of conversations, refilling drinks, talking about current events, politics, and mostly about law.

Janet spoke briefly with her father-in-law and then drifted over to the edge of the room, listening to the noise, the clink of glasses, the coughs, the talk. Mary joined her in a moment, and silently they watched their husbands.

Wiley and Tim were amazing. They were working the room, poised and polished, a smile here, a touch of ironic wit there. Wiley was smiling, agreeing, yes, that he thought teaching a challenge, that legal education needed some reform, nothing too drastic, of course, just a few changes here and there.

If he straightened his tie once or twice too

often, only Janet noticed. And whatever small signs revealed Tim's inner turmoil needed Mary to recognize.

They were locked into their best professional manner. The whole room was.

Soon the gathering moved into the larger banquet room, everyone finding his place at the round white-covered tables. Janet was seated between two of her father-in-law's colleagues. They asked her how she was, she said that she was fine; she asked them how they were, they said that they were fine. Then they ignored her.

She didn't mind. Every so often she glanced at Mary, who was in exactly the same situation a few tables away, but soon she had to stop doing that or the pair of them would have started to laugh.

After dinner there were a few toasts, although they certainly sounded like speeches to Janet. Wiley's father gave one. It was no different than the rest, a few jokes about David Franklin, a few more about retirement. The evening seemed like a colossal waste of time to Janet, but she knew it wasn't. The lawyers were all picking up on news, making contacts, thinking just as much about business on Saturday night as they might on a Tuesday morning.

As soon as people started to leave, Mary got up. She tilted her head and briefly rested her cheek on her folded hands, signaling to Janet that she was tired. She went to Tim and touched his arm, clearly telling him that she wanted to leave.

Janet knew what would happen. Tim would smile and nod at her, but go right on talking. Mary would wait, shifting from one foot to another. Finally he would start moving to the door, but then someone else would stop him and ... Janet had been through it a million times.

But she was wrong. Within moments, Tim took Mary's arm and, like any normal human being, walked out the door.

How nice.

Janet looked around the room for Wiley, wondering if you had to be pregnant to have that trick work.

She spotted him talking to a man about his father's age. The man moved a little and she saw Wiley's face. He seemed animated, enthusiastic.

This wasn't the polished manner. He was excited about something. But what could it be? What could anyone here tell him that would excite him? He was out of all this.

After a bit the other man excused himself, and Wiley started looking around the room. Janet hoped he was looking for her.

Indeed he was. As soon as he caught sight of her, he came over quickly.

"You look like a happy duck," she said as he sat down in the chair next to her. "What was that all about?"

"That was Unc—Jack Paige."

"Were you about to call him Uncle Jack?"

Wiley smiled almost sheepishly. "That's what I called him as a kid, although he's not my uncle or anything. He's pretty tight with the governor and some party officials."

Anyone who had been a close enough friend of Lee Hunt for Wiley to call the man "uncle" was bound to be tight with the governor and some party officials. At a minimum.

"Anyway, he was sounding me out about a job, an appointment on the governor's staff."

Janet frowned, confused. Wiley already had a job; he was going to teach. "But, Wiley, I thought you didn't want to work in government, and this is state government."

"It's not the same; let me finish. The governor's almost sure to run for Senate next year, and they want to bring me on to start research policy matters and then once the campaign starts, I'd be issues director."

"A campaign? You?"

A campaign. Janet felt sick. She remembered campaigns from when she worked for her congressman. He had a safe seat, and still the campaigns were exhausting, wearing, numbing. And a Senate campaign in New York. It would be everything awful. The long hours, the stress, the traveling. Surely Wiley wouldn't choose this over the law school job. She looked at him, searching his face for signs that he wouldn't.

But there was a current surging through him, an electric surge that she knew too well from her first years at the agency, the irresistible lure of work, of challenging, satisfying work.

Oh, Lord . . .

"Are you really interested in getting involved in politics?" she asked. "You've never . . . you've never before expressed any interest in it."

He laughed. "It's a change for me, isn't it? But working on this book has . . . I don't know. I used to be pretty arrogant, I guess. Asking people for their votes used to seem degrading, but I don't know why it should. Just because people don't have law degrees doesn't mean they can't make intelligent decisions if they have decent information, if they—'' He stopped and laughed again. He put his arm across the back of her chair. "I'm sounding like you, aren't I?"

Oh, no, please, no. I don't ever want to sound like this again. Yes, yes, this feeling, this craving for work, is wonderful, it's sharper, more intense than anything else, but it consumes, it leaves you obsessed, self-absorbed.

"You're really considering this, aren't you?" she had to say.

He drew back, startled. "Oh, Janet, don't you see what an opportunity this is—to be really involved again. It's a dream come true."

The table had already been cleared. Just a few silver-bordered coffee cups remained; some had pink lipstick smudges on the rims.

Janet had thought their dreams already were coming true. Less demanding jobs, a house, walks after dinner, a life of their own. That had been her dream. But apparently it had only been second-best for him.

He was still looking at her, concerned, trying to understand her reluctance. She didn't know what to say and spoke almost at random. "Will your office be in New York City?" How she would hate to live in the city.

"Yes." Then he seemed suddenly relieved. "Was that what you were worried about? That it would be up in Albany? No, the state has some offices here. I made that clear right away, that you would need to be in the city. I never expected you to give up your career for mine, but New York is where all the big ad agencies are. You can really go for the big time if you want. You won't have to put up with all the aggravations of a small agency, of being understaffed, of doing things on the cheap." He paused, looking down at her. "This is all right, isn't it? A couple of years in New York, and then if he wins, we could go back to Washington, and you could write your own ticket at any Washington agency. This could be as good for your career as it is for mine. I wouldn't consider it otherwise."

Don't think about my career; think about me.

"But we don't have to move," he said quickly, obviously wanting to give her career every possible consideration. "Not if you don't want to leave the agency. I can commute; it probably wouldn't matter a lot, since I'll be traveling so much anyway."

Traveling . . .

"No," she said slowly. "I'll come with you."

But at that moment, she wasn't at all sure why.

None of it had made any difference to him; none of it at all. His leaving the firm, his being home, their writing the book together, their now being able to talk about Column A and Column B— none of it mattered to him. If Wiley could have wiped out the last six months, if he could have been a driven, exhausted Hastings & Clark associate again, he would have done it.

But he had changed. She was sure of that. Six

months ago he would have considered himself above politics; politicians have to worry about everyone with a voter registration card. Hastings & Clark attorneys need not bother with such ordinary people. And six months ago, Wiley wouldn't have worried so much about her job, about how a move would affect her career—after all, she was in advertising, he would have thought six months ago, how could that compare to law?

To the man she had already loved and admired, the last six months had added humility and sympathy—traits that Midwestern Janet valued with every breath that she took. They were all she had ever felt lacking in his character; now he had changed.

But clearly not enough. She had been so sure, so very sure, that he had learned what she had, that nothing, not work, not success, not anything, can be as satisfying as the rich intimacies of marriage. Of course, marriage was not enough by itself, no one thing in life ever is enough, but marriage could be the center, the core around which all else spun.

But if Wiley took this job, within another six months they'd be right back where they were, making their work the center of their lives, sacrificing everything for their jobs.

How could he? How *could* he?

Chapter Fourteen

"Do you believe it?" Wiley was saying in the taxi on the way home. "You know, you were right, I was dreading this evening. Who would have thought it would have turned out like this?"

Yes, who would have?

Wiley had his hands laced behind his neck; his legs were stretched out, his feet propped up on the jump seat that was folded down on the floor of the cab. He seemed very distant.

Get used to it, Janet told herself. *Because it's going to get worse.*

She sat there dumbly, silently, miserably, until at last just as they were nearing Wiley's father's house, she realized what she was doing.

She wasn't talking to him. She wasn't telling him what she was thinking. God knows she had done that for nearly eight years and it had gotten them nowhere. From the very beginning, they hadn't talked. She had never said why she wanted to get married; he had never said why he didn't. They never talked about when they would have children. They never talked about anything that mattered. They couldn't.

But at last they had learned how to talk to one another, talk without so much defensiveness, so much evasiveness and confusion. Why was she instantly reverting to the old ways?

"Listen, Wiley, I've got one reservation about this new job."

He looked at her. "Is it living in New York? We don't have to live in the city; some of the suburbs are nice."

Great, and add an hour commute to a twelve-hour work day.

But she didn't say that; that was pointless sarcasm; it would get them nowhere. And in the trading pointless sarcasm sweepstakes, Wiley could sneer circles around her.

"No, we can work all that out later. I'm concerned about what this will do to our marriage."

"Our marriage?" He looked startled, confused.

"Don't you remember what things were like this winter? When it seemed like our marriage was over?"

"Yes, but we're beyond that. I mean—" Suddenly he faltered. "Janet...it's never been like this before...I..."

She understood how hard this was for him—the Hastings & Clark style did not extend to telling your wife how close you felt to her—but at least Wiley had let the flowers on the train and his mother's opals speak for him.

"We've never been this close," she finished for him. "But I worry that this job will ruin all that, that we'll end up right back where we were last year."

"Oh." And he was quiet. Then at last, "I won't

do anything impulsive, you know that. I mean, nothing's certain on their end and we'll certainly talk it all through before I commit myself.''

"I think that that is important."

He was quiet, thinking about what she said. Then something occurred to him and he turned to her, speaking quickly. "But, Janet, don't you think we'll be all right because we've learned to talk to each other? Don't you think that all the good things that have happened will be enough to sustain us through a demanding job?"

Her heart sank. Obviously he wanted this job so much that he was reaching desperately for any argument that would convince her—and himself—that he should take it.

"Well, it might," she said uncertainly, unconvinced. Work, success, was like a drug, enticing, irresistible, killing. "But is that the kind of life we really want?"

"We'll still love each other."

But the cab pulled up to the curb and the driver looked over his shoulder, so Janet didn't have a chance to remind Wiley that they had always loved each other, but love hadn't always been enough.

Lee Hunt had left the banquet earlier than they had, but he was still up when they came into the house. He stepped into the foyer.

"I was just taking out some brandy," he said. "Can I talk you into some?"

"My arm is yours for the twisting," Wiley replied, light, ironic, the perfect lawyer. Or was it the perfect politician now?

In the living room, Lee lifted the heavy crystal decanter in her direction. "Janet?"

"Nothing for me, thanks. I think I'll go to bed."

"Yes," Lee agreed. "It was a long evening."

Then suddenly, as absorbed as she was in her own unhappiness, Janet realized something that had been flitting at the edge of her perception all evening—her father-in-law had been acting strangely.

Well, not really strange, just a little different. But given the very narrow range of behavior permitted to Wall Street lawyers, acting just a little differently was out at the limit.

Yes, he had worked the room all evening with the same professional polish that he had passed on to his son, but when he had spoken to Janet, when he had taken her hand, he had not noticed the opals or mentioned Janet and Wiley's anniversary.

Lee Hunt was excellent at birthdays and anniversaries. Janet always got flowers on her birthday, Wiley got a phone call on his, and on their anniversary, they invariably received a piece of silver that they never used.

In fact, Lee was better about sending gifts on time than Janet's parents were. Generally, Peg Barnum would remember about halfway through the day, when she was writing a check at the grocery store, and then would have to make a frantic, flurried phone call.

But the difference was that Peg remembered the date and it got remembered for Lee. Janet knew that he had a calendar with such dates marked in it; each year his secretary would transcribe them into his new calendar and then note them on her own so that she could alert him when they approached.

So Janet was not hurt that he didn't wish her happy anniversary or have a gift for her. It just seemed surprising that the system had failed.

She thought it even odder that he had not noticed the opals. He had bought them, for heaven's sake, giving them to Wiley's mother to wear on their wedding day. Surely he would remember that without having it written on his calendar. But he had told her she looked lovely in the most routine way, not even giving the opals a second glance.

Janet had always thought of her father-in-law as a monolith, impenetrable, invulnerable, incomprehensible. But he was bothered by something. She wished she knew what it was, she'd like to help.

So instead of going to bed, she sat down on the camel-backed sofa, waiting quietly.

Wiley and his father had gone over to a pair of wing chairs, upholstered in a tobacco-colored leather. As they set their brandy snifters down on the small mahogany butler's tray, Lee spoke.

"I shared a cab home with Jack Paige."

Wiley's eyes went swiftly to his father's, asking.

"He told me," Lee confirmed. "Son, that's wonderful news."

Wiley's smile was quick, light. "I was wondering if I could say something to you. He said to keep it quiet."

"Not that quiet," Lee returned.

"So you think it's a good opportunity."

"Most definitely. Not only will you be doing something important, providing a real service to the people of New York, but if he's elected, you'll have a chance to work at making some important changes—"

Oh, no, that's not it. Janet suddenly felt hostile. *What really matters to both of you is that Wiley will be back at it, out doing the Hunt name proud.*

They looked so alike sitting there, leaning back in their traditional chairs, legs crossed, hands curled around their brandy glasses.

"In fact," Lee went on, "if things had been different, if your mother hadn't been so concerned about security, I might have taken a job like this—"

I can't compete against this. If it were just the work, maybe he would be right, that the closeness we've built up might have given us some defenses. But this is his father's approval we're talking about here, and there's no way I can compete with that.

Janet no longer cared about anyone's misery except her own. She stood up, about to excuse herself. The men paid no attention.

"In fact," Lee was saying, "I rather envy you—starting off on something as exciting as this."

And then with that inexplicable intuition that made her able to write ads that comforted people's fears, Janet understood. She understood why Lee hadn't noticed the opals, why even when she had returned home, he still hadn't noticed them, and why when he had spoken of Wiley's opportunities a moment ago, he had resembled

Wiley, but not the bright-eyed Wiley of this evening, but Wiley in March, grim and dispirited. She understood what was wrong.

Her anger, her sense of being ill-used, dissolved in a flow of sympathy.

And she sat down, waiting patiently as father and son talked, about Wiley's marvelous chances, his great future.

At last they seemed to have said enough, and Wiley stood and came to her. "Are you ready to go to bed?"

She got up and spoke directly to Lee, something which she generally avoided doing. "Have you been feeling all right?"

Wiley looked at her oddly. Clearly he hadn't noticed anything at all strange about his father's behavior.

"I'm fine, thank you," Lee told her. "But it is late, and—"

And then Janet did what she would have never dreamed of doing, not to Wiley's father. She interrupted him, and she contradicted him. "No, you aren't. Something's been bothering you." And she knew what it was.

Lee looked at her in surprise, his eyes seeming to take a moment to focus on her. "It's nothing—" He stopped and then swiveled his head toward Wiley. "Those are your mother's opals."

"Oh, blast," Wiley cursed. "I meant to tell you last night, but when you had to cancel dinner, I forgot—"

How symbolic, Janet thought sadly, *one more canceled dinner.*

"—I hope it is all right."

"Oh, certainly." Lee came over to Janet and lifted a hand to touch the pendant gently. "I remember buying these. She—" He stopped, clearing his throat. "I hope you enjoy wearing them."

"I will," Janet promised, wondering, for the first time, if Wiley's mother had been a happy woman.

And then perhaps because he was still standing so close and she could speak softly, she asked, "Lee,"—she had probably never used his name before—"what happened tonight? What was wrong?"

Wiley stepped nearer, trying to hear.

"I just don't like affairs like that, that's all," Lee answered.

"Because it was for a retirement?"

Lee smiled at her, his practiced, political smile. He did not answer. He did not want to discuss it.

Janet persisted. "When do you retire?"

"I'm sixty-four. We can leave at sixty-five; we have to leave at sixty-eight."

"Are you making plans?"

"A few. What about your father?" Lee changed the subject. "I suppose in a private practice like his, no one can force you to retire."

"No," Janet acknowledged. "But he's going to retire at the end of next year. He's ambivalent; he's loved it, but having a large animal practice is hard work, your nights and weekends get interrupted. So he's looking forward to time with Mother. They're getting a camper and plan to travel a lot."

"Well, he still has your mother." Lee's voice had an empty sound, and he stepped away, turning back to the marble-topped server to pour himself more brandy. A little rainbow of light sparkled off the crystal facets of the decanter.

Wiley spoke quickly, softly. "What's going on?"

Couldn't he tell? "Your father's afraid of retirement."

"Dad?" Wiley was surprised. "Afraid? What could he be afraid of?"

That's what seven-year-olds say: "My Daddy ain't scared of nothing."

"What does he have in his life but his job?" she asked.

"Why, his friends, his—"

Wiley broke off; Lee had rejoined them.

"What are your plans, Dad?" Wiley's mask was back in place; he asked the question as if he had only the mildest curiosity.

"I'll probably do some writing, some teaching."

"Wait a minute," Wiley responded lightly. "That's what I planned on doing, and I'm not retired."

"That's right," Janet said. "You shouldn't just exchange one job for another."

"Don't you want to spend summers up in Maine?" Wiley asked. "Isn't that what you and Mother always talked about?"

Lee shrugged. "I don't really know the people up there. It was your mother who did. I haven't spent much time up there since she died."

Then he set down his unfinished brandy. Lee Hunt, who had faced down Iranian bankers and United States senators, could not endure this conversation. Gracefully, smoothly, he said good night to his son and daughter-in-law and left the room.

Wiley turned to Janet. "How did you know?"

"It stands to reason. He has no hobbies, no interests outside work. His friends are all professional associates. He might have managed if your mother had lived; she was probably his link to the rest of the world. But he's on his own now."

"He'll do fine," Wiley asserted too quickly. "He always does everything well."

Janet shook her head. "Wiley, your father is a fabulous lawyer, but name me one other thing he has done well."

"Janet!" This was heresy; she could see that in his eyes. "How can you say that?"

"Name one."

"Well, there's the most obvious one; he's been an excellent father."

Janet said nothing. Through the muffling swath of velvet drape, a siren wailed faintly.

At last she spoke. "Keep trying; you'll never get me to buy that one."

Wiley turned restlessly, unused to the narrowness of a twin bed.

What on earth had Janet meant? That she'd never buy that one? Was she suggesting that his father hadn't—

Yes, of course, that's what she was saying.

Well, she was wrong; that's all, wrong. Sure, his dad hadn't been the same sort of father that Dick Barnum had been, taking his kids out to watch calves being born, forcing them to help paint the church basement. If that was what good fathers did, then he was just as happy to have passed on the pleasure, thank you.

Wiley had such wonderful memories of his father, the first sailing lessons and then the first time Wiley had beaten him at golf, how pleased he had been, all those wonderful memories of times when Wiley had earned that "Well done, son."

How could anyone say he hadn't been a good father?

Janet was just upset. This new job offer had surprised her, and then all this business with Mary and Tim, that had been stressful.

Mary...

Mary's father had drifted in and out of her life. He had never been around. He had been "half a father." She must have no memories of doing things with him. Not like the memories Wiley had of his father helping him with his tennis serve, of ... of—

Dan was worried about it too, about being half a father or even less than that. If his daughter grew up in California, she would hardly know Dan. She too would have no memories of her father.

Not like the memories Wiley had, the wonderful memories.

Of an hour of tennis on Sunday or a quick round of golf. An afternoon sail before his father went back to New York for the week. And the time that ... that ... what time?

Frantically Wiley tried to pull together the memories of his earliest years. Evenings at home, Saturday mornings, something, but he kept coming up with nothing.

The memories were all of his mother, coming to school assemblies, helping him with his homework, writing letters to him at camp. Until junior high, when the golf and sailing started, when he was old enough to eat dinner at nine o'clock when his parents did, Wiley had no memories of his father. None.

Because Wiley D. Hunt hadn't been around either. Because he had been at work.

"Janet!"

Wiley hardly realized he'd spoken aloud. He glanced over at the other bed, afraid that he had woken her up.

She hadn't been sleeping either and was already sitting up. "What is it, Wiley?"

He wasn't sure what he had wanted to tell her. "Why don't you come over here?"

She slipped out of her bed and crossed over to his. Her nightgown was yellow, a bright daffodil, and as he moved over, making room for her, he felt it ride up as she slid down in bed. Her legs were warm against his.

She started to pull the nightgown down.

"Don't do that," he said. "Unless it's uncomfortable."

"No."

He had his arm around her and she curled up against him; her feathery hair was soft against his shoulder. He could feel her breathe, the steady rise and fall of her warmth beside him. And he remembered the one Browning poem his mother hadn't wanted to hear that summer, the last summer of her life: Grow old along with me!/The best is yet to be . . . .

Stay with me, Janet. Don't let me turn out like him, alone and afraid.

"Janet?"

"What is it?" They were both speaking very low.

"Last winter, when you said you weren't sure if you wanted children anymore, was it because you were afraid I would be the same sort of parent my father was?"

It took her a moment before she decided what to say and then it was simple. "Yes."

"Are you still worried about it?" Surely she wasn't, not after this spring, not after —

"Yes."

And he must have looked surprised, puzzled, for she went on. "Yesterday, Lord, even this morning, I wasn't; I thought we were going to be all right, but this evening, the minute someone gave you a chance to be your father again, you took it, you grabbed at it . . . this job, Wiley, this new job," she explained. "It's your chance to be your dad again."

Oh.

She was sitting up now, facing him, her arms wrapped around her knees. "Don't you see? He's still this vague ideal you're trying to imitate, this god you're trying to please. The four of us don't feel that way about Daddy. We love him, but he's human and we don't knock ourselves out to please him now. You still feel as much pressure to win your father's approval as you did at eleven because that's the only way he knew how to approach you, by giving or withholding his approval. He loved you, but he didn't know how to show it, and by itself like that, love isn't enough."

Janet's words came to him slowly, like the light of a cloudy day finding its way through the panes of a leaded glass window. But the light is no less true because it has traveled so far. And Wiley too could see the pattern of his life.

Yes, he had wanted to be like his father. More than anything he had wanted to be like his father.

But things kept happening: his mother, Janet, and that pile of blue powder out in Western Iowa.

He had gone to Georgetown rather than let his mother die alone, he had snuffed out his career rather than let the nation lose a section of farmland, he had married the sort of woman he never thought he would marry.

Each one of these had thrown his life off his father's course, and the three together probably represented the best things that he, as a human being, had ever done.

Yet every time, in every single case, he had done all that he could to get back on track.

At Georgetown he had killed himself to be at the top of his class, he had sacrificed everything, including learning, to make sure his grades would compensate for his not being at Harvard or Yale.

Then with Janet, yes, he really had held back from her, keeping himself removed, distant. He hadn't wanted to be a Barnum—noisy, spontaneous, generous, selfless—so he hadn't been a husband either.

And finally with the job. What he had done last winter had been right, not just because of the farmland, but it had been personally right. He had walked away from a job that consumed him, that left him with only one soul-side, the side that he

faced the world with; he had been about to take
another job that would leave him with time to be
something more than a lawyer. But at the last
minute, he had been offered a chance to be his
father again. And he had taken it.

"Do you think I'll end up like him?" he asked
Janet, knowing the answer.

"It doesn't matter what I think. It matters what
you think."

"But I'll have you," he said, protesting, plead-
ing.

She shook her head, and he remembered what
she had said in the cab—that this new job was
likely to take them back to where they were a year
ago—on the road to divorce.

But she said something else. "No, I could die
tomorrow."

Yes, the wedding ceremony was pretty blunt
about that one: "Until death us do part."

"All the time," she went on, "people complain
that women depend too much on men for money,
social position, that whole Cinderella business,
but I think men depend too much on women.
We're the ones who tell you what you're feeling,
we're the ones who remind you that there's
something in life besides work. Don't depend on
me to rescue you from the consequences of your
own decisions. I'll try to, I'll always try to, but I
might not always be able."

The glow from the streetlight outside his window filtered through the curtains to give the room
a gray half-light. Janet looked sober, serious.

Was it already too late? She must feel very betrayed. They had been so close to the kind of life

she had wanted and suddenly he had pulled back from it.

Last winter she had said that she didn't trust him, that there would always be another U.S. Oil. And this evening he had proved her right, hadn't he?

He had said he thought their marriage would survive a return to more demanding jobs. "Perhaps," she had said, "but is that the kind of life we want?"

Hastings & Clark had been a great job, but it hadn't made for much of a life—coming home so late that Janet was already asleep, loosening his tie as he stood in front of the almost-empty refrigerator, wondering if he should bother to eat. The bright little bulb in the refrigerator would be the only light in the cold, dark apartment.

And Wiley was suddenly just as certain as he had been each time before, when he had wanted to be with his mother, when he had married Janet, when he had gone to EPA; he was just as sure that no, that was not the kind of life he wanted.

He wanted what Janet wanted, not what his father wanted.

It was possible to excel at one thing—that was the course his father had chosen, but when you try to do two things, then you have to compromise.

Janet had chosen the path of compromise. She could have had an important position at any of the largest advertising agencies or she could have been Homemaker of the Year, but instead she had decided to be both wife and worker, and she knew that she'd do both less than perfectly. But her life would be fuller, richer, because she had rejected a single-minded pursuit.

He could compromise too. He could change. He didn't need to have a high-powered, visible job. Not when he had Janet, not since he had learned what she had taught him about intimacy.

"Janet, you know I love you, don't you?"

"Of course."

"Do you also know that I admire you more than anyone I've ever met?"

She blinked in surprise. "Admire me? You admire me? Why?"

"Because you're the most sensible person I know."

She frowned, confused. "That's not what you say when you want me to plan investments."

"No, no, I don't mean that. I'm talking about ... well, about emotional things. You know how to manage them. Everyone we know works too hard, is too absorbed and obsessed by their work—"

"I was too. Last winter I was too."

"I know, that's my point. You were too, but of everyone, you were the only one who knew how to get out of it. The Keanes, the Stewarts, and us—all our marriages were in a mess last winter, but you and I are going to come out the best ... and it's because you knew how."

Janet shrugged. "Wiley, don't be so confident that things are going to be all right with us. I mean, things are better than they have ever been, but that's because we—both of us, you as well as me—have been working as hard at our marriage as we used to work on our jobs, but—"

He shook his head. "I'm taking the teaching job; it's what's right for me, for us. I know I lapsed this evening, I know I was overwhelmed by ambition again, but it's hard, when you've always been taught that you're one thing, to start thinking of yourself as another."

She nodded. "I still feel a little guilty because I don't sew my own clothes; I probably always will."

"Well, if you can't get it quite right, I suppose I'll never come close, but all I can do is try."

"Being happy is hard work."

He lifted his hand, brushed some of the soft curls off her forehead. "I didn't know that. I thought happiness just came ... if you married the right woman, if you were successful, that was all you had to do, then you'd be happy."

She shook her head. "It's not that easy."

"We did almost make ourselves very unhappy, but from here on, we're going to concentrate on making ourselves happy, not just successful, but happy too."

Fortunately for this resolve, Janet did not die the next day. Quite the contrary. She and Wiley spent the weekend eating their way through New York with such a festive lack of caution that she returned to Washington to find that she had gained two-and-a-half pounds. But that was nothing. By the end of the year, she—with Wiley's help—embarked on a little project that would doom her to quite a considerable weight gain.

Mary Keane had her baby first, of course. She took six weeks off work and made elaborate arrangements so she could go back. She and Tim found a treasure of a woman who loved the baby, who did the dishes and the laundry, who would come early and stay late, and who could almost speak English. It seemed like an ideal arrangement.

Four months later, to the surprise of all who knew her, Mary fired the "treasure"—or rather bestowed her upon an envious friend—and quit her job altogether. She wanted to be with her baby, especially as Tim still traveled more than a father really should.

Tim was now a partner at Hastings & Clark. Of the three senior associates who had boarded that plane in Houston last February, only he had gotten his partnership. His income was a joke; he and Mary did not have time to spend all the money that he made.

Tim dearly loved the baby, a little boy who looked like no one but his chubby-cheeked self. But whatever the child looked like, his six-month pictures were quite a different matter. Tim's mother smiled when she saw them, dug through her bureau and pulled out Tim's own baby book. The pictures of the two babies were interchangeable.

The new grandma thought this rather sweet, but, on the whole, not very surprising. She never did understand why Tim pulled the book from her so roughly.

"It didn't really make a difference," Mary told Janet later. "We knew he was Tim's, we knew right away. It was obvious when you thought about the timing. I can't imagine why I was ever worried about it."

And Janet thought that this sentiment revealed a great deal about the resiliency of human emotions and nothing at all about Mary's and Tim's analytic abilities.

Lee Hunt did retire from his law firm in a few years, but he had arranged other work for himself so he wouldn't have to be retired. It was a less demanding job, but his life suddenly took on the most unexpected challenge. A casually said "Let me know what I can do" resulted in Wiley and Janet depositing their three-year-old into his care for twenty-four hours.

It was an extraordinary day for him. He did things for Katherine that he had never done for his own child and he did nothing that day but those things. For the first time in his adult life, he did not have a chance to read the newspaper. He got up when Katie did, he ate when she did, he took a nap when she did—needing it a great deal more than she did, by the way—and when Wiley and Janet came to retrieve her, he sighed and said, "How do women manage? Especially when they have more than one."

Even though he was not completely retired, he had more time for his granddaughter than he had ever had for his son, and he was more keenly aware of how very much he loved the little girl. One day he even discovered himself asking Janet how long they had to wait before giving Katie her grandmother's mink coat.

"It depends on what you want her to do with it," Janet answered. Katie was just starting to play dress-up.

Wiley and Janet had found a nice house for

themselves, a blue-shuttered Dutch colonial near the old Glen Echo amusement park. It was a quick commute to the law school, which Wiley loved, and it was on a pretty wooded lot, which Janet loved.

At least she loved her trees until she tried to plant a garden. Janet might have been ready to cultivate her own garden, but her tomatoes did not get enough sun.

Fortunately, she managed other parts of her life better than she did her garden. She decided to profit from Mary's experience and so before her baby was born, she turned over her position as senior writer to someone else and became a part-time consultant to the agency. She breezed in, had great ideas, and then left. At least that was how it was supposed to work. Sometimes it was hard to leave, sometimes her ideas weren't so great, but enough of them still were that no one complained. Except Alan Rule, but that was to be expected.

It would be lovely to say that Wiley Hunt turned into the ideal husband and father, generous with his time, ever ready to sacrifice his professional interests to those of his wife and child, his community and church, but, of course, he did not. He liked living in a house, he enjoyed walking the dog after dinner, he was crazy about his daughter, but he paid someone else to clean the gutters and mow the lawn, and he still had occasional fits when he would be working on an article and suddenly it would turn interesting, and he'd be just as obsessed as ever.

But such fits were only occasional now, and

when they passed, he would look up and think that it really hadn't been worth it.

And whenever Wiley thought that, whenever he would think how fortunate he was that he had a family and a home, instead of just an office and an expense account, whenever he'd feel blessed that his life was no longer like his father's, he always remembered to tell Janet.

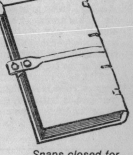